TILL I END MY SONG

ENGLISH MUSIC AND MUSICIANS

1440 – 1940

A PERSPECTIVE FROM ETON

The Chapel from the South East

TILL I END MY SONG

ENGLISH MUSIC AND MUSICIANS
1440 – 1940

A PERSPECTIVE FROM ETON

RICHARD OSBORNE

*To Ken
with every best wish

Richard*

THE CYGNET PRESS

Frontispiece: *Eton College Chapel from the South East*
by F. L. Griggs, 1910
Reproduced by kind permission
of the artist's daughter, Barbara van der Zee

Published in Great Britain by
The Cygnet Press
187 Fentiman Road, London s w 8 1 j y

ISBN 0 907435 16 5

Printed and bound by Biddles Ltd
King's Lynn, Norfolk

Sweete Themmes runne softly, till I end my Song

Edmund Spenser, *Prothalamion*

CONTENTS

CHAPTER I

Choirbook

In 1441, Thomas Bekynton, Secretary to King Henry VI, journeyed to Rome via the port of Bordeaux to negotiate the granting of Papal Bulls on behalf of Henry's newly-founded 'College Roiall of Our Ladie of Eton beside Windesor'. The sea crossing was strangely tranquil, threatening to delay the embassy. Nothing daunted, Bekynton

… vowed an offering to the Blessed Virgin of Eton, and persuaded some of his companions to do likewise. They all then joined in an antiphon in her honour; after which, we are told, a favourable wind arose.

Fact or legend, it is a representative tale. Prayer transfigured by the power of music was central to the idea of Eton as Henry VI originally conceived it.

It has often been asked why Henry, having elected to found a chantry-cum-school within sight of his birthplace at Windsor, chose to establish it in Eton rather than on more salubrious ground in Windsor Great Park. Good approach-roads and an assured water-supply would have commended Eton to the king's advisers. More relevant to his own private purpose, however, was the existence in Eton of a parish church dedicated to the Assumption of the Blessed Virgin; a church, moreover, which already taught and maintained singing boys.

In the Royal Charter by which Eton was established in October 1440 there is mention of 'six chorister boys', a reflection, in all probability, of the situation inherited by

Henry. By the time the first statutes were drawn up, Henry's plans had been put on an altogether grander footing. In addition to the Provost and his 'college of sad priests', there were to be sixteen choristers alongside seventy so-called poor and indigent scholars. It is worth noting, however, that *in extremis* the scholars could be dispensed with. In July 1455, Henry ordered an addendum to the statutes, charging the Provost and Fellows, on pain of punishment for perjury, with completing the minster church in the event of his death and maintaining within it four chaplains, four clerks (one of them to be skilled in playing the organ) and eight choristers. There is no mention of the scholars in this addendum.

The original statutes were drawn up by the Lincolnshire-born William Waynflete, recruited from Winchester to be Eton's first schoolmaster and, within months of his arrival, its second Provost. William of Wykeham's New College, Oxford (1379) and its sister foundation Winchester College (1394) were Henry's models, though the idea of a double foundation of his own did not finally take shape until the summer of 1441 when he approved the foundation of King's College, Cambridge to receive the 'annual ripe fruit' of mature young Eton scholars.

Though the Eton statutes were closely based on the Winchester model, the particular concern they show for the choristers indicates a changed aesthetic and altered priorities. Statute XIV decreed that the choristers be given the same schooling as the scholars, not as a courtesy, but to allow preferential access to scholarships for those choristers who had proved themselves proficient in reading, chanting, and the rudiments of Latin grammar. Conversely, foundation scholars who were not choristers were required to be sufficiently gifted musically to be capable of deputising for choristers who might be unavoidably absent. Most remarkable of all were the conditions governing the appointment of the Master of the Choristers. In addition to being a skilled musician, he was required to possess a wide-ranging knowledge of non-musical matters. It was also recommended that he be married. This last recommendation, which reads more like a provision of some late-twentieth-century child-care regulation than a statute relating to a quasi-ecclesiastical foundation of the mid-fifteenth century, was said to be for the 'protection and domestic comfort' of the boys.

As Miss Maria Hackett, the nineteenth-century's most tireless campaigner for choirs and choir-schools, would later insist: 'ETON COLLEGE as originally constituted by the Royal Founder may be regarded as the noblest MUSIC SCHOOL in the kingdom'.

*

The elaborate religious life of the community, with its roster of daily services, seven of them masses, said or sung (though not yet polyphonically) was first established in the parish church adjacent to what, throughout the 1440s, was a large building site. By the end of the decade, a schoolroom, accommodation for the scholars, and a grand yet companionable College Hall had been completed. There was, however, dismay at the state of the College church which had been demolished in 1449 when Henry drew up revised plans to build a minster as grand as any in the land. Had the College been permanently suppressed after Henry's deposition by Edward IV, little would have remained of the church other than architects' drawings and the half-finished shell of a lavishly endowed building. Happily, this did not happen. In July 1455, citing pressure of work, though, more likely, alarmed by his own fragile mental state, Henry delegated responsibility for Eton and its statutes to Waynflete.[1] A priest and politician by occupation but an educator by inclination, Waynflete was ideally equipped to continue the work he himself had partly started. An attempt was made in 1465, four years after Henry's deposition, to transfer Eton's properties to St George's, Windsor (a move bravely resisted by the new Provost, William Westbury) but Waynflete himself had little difficulty in coming to terms with the new regime whilst at the same time actively pursuing his own modified version of Henry's vision of Eton.

In 1469, Waynflete determined to complete the Eton church by adding, largely at his own expense, a small ante-chapel to the existing half-finished choir, a move designed as much to placate the parish, whose church this also was, as to aggrandise the college.[2] Waynflete's determination to see the building finished, and the election as Provost in 1477 of wheeler-dealing court favourite, Henry Bost, helped drive the project forward. Work on the famous wall paintings at the parishioners' end of the church would continue until 1487, and the exquisitely fan-vaulted chantry chapel would not be added until 1515, but the new church was effectively ready for occupation by 1479-80. It proved to be a timely completion, and not only for Eton.

*

The earliest English composer to be revered by his contempo-

1 Waynflete had left Eton in 1447 to become Bishop of Winchester. In 1456, Henry appointed him Lord Chancellor.
2 The ante-chapel was used by Eton parishioners until 1769.

raries in England and abroad was John Dunstable (*c*.1390-1453). Since subsequent generations knew all too little of his music, it was routinely assumed that English music first flourished a century later with the music of Tallis, Byrd, and Gibbons. That there was an earlier flowering, we now know from two sources: our fuller knowledge of Dunstable's music and the chance survival of a unique anthology of pre-Reformation English church music, the Eton Choirbook.

Numerous choirbooks existed at the time. The Chapel Royal, King's College, Cambridge, Magdalen College, Oxford, St George's, Windsor all possessed comparable volumes. None of these has survived. Had the Eton Choirbook also been lost or destroyed, the loss would have been grievous. Between 1480, when Eton's church and choir finally came fully into their own, and 1515, when Robert Wylkynson (*c*.1450-?1515) died or retired as Master of the Choristers, English music advanced as it had not done before and as it has rarely done since in so short a space of time. What began as simple-sounding compositions took on, within the space of three decades, a hitherto undreamed of reach and complexity.

Since fifteenth-century choristers would normally learn and rehearse their music from manuscript rolls, the great choirbooks were not so much working volumes as fair copies of a choir's repertory. Grand atlas-size folios (the Eton Choirbook measures 24 x 17 inches), their function was partly mnemonic, partly ceremonial. The Eton Choirbook is particularly handsome. Copied onto the finest vellum, the penmanship is elegant, the illumination superb. The large number of illustrated initials at the heads of staves, separately designed then painted and pasted in, are of interest both for the

5

Englishness of their subject-matter and their occasional bursts of humour. Brown owls feature a good deal, a reference, it is thought, to the composer Browne. Of particular interest is the illustrated initial in Wylkynson's 'O Virgo prudentissima' which pictures an exquisitely drawn grey sea-shell in a blaze of sunlight on a field of green: a whelk-in-the-sun or 'Wylkynson'.

Who paid for the Eton Choirbook is not known, though it is unlikely to have been the College itself. A possible donor is Walter Smythe (d.1524), one of the unsung heroes of Eton's early years. Bibliophile, benefactor, and convinced vegetarian, Smythe had been College Precentor in the Choirbook's heyday and later served as Vice-Provost.[3] The epitaph on his tombstone reads: 'This perpetual fellow led an honest life at Eton; a moderate man whose food was beans; among the virtues in which he shone, he relieved misery of the poor, and he cultivated music.'

★

Visitors from abroad in the early years of the sixteenth century often remarked on the quality of the singing they experienced in English churches. Erasmus disapproved: 'A set of creatures who ought to be lamenting their sins fancy they can please God by gurgling in their throats. Boys are kept in the English Benedictine colleges solely and simply to sing hymns to the Virgin'. Others marvelled. 'More divine than human' was the judgment of one awe-struck visitor.

A traveller arriving in Eton c.1500 might have thought

3 As Precentor, Smythe would have been responsible for the church's liturgy and its music. The position of Masters of the Choristers (one of the functions of latter-day Precentors) was entirely separate.

likewise had he paused to worship in the new minster church on one of the great Feast Days or, lodging nearby, entered the church at dusk. The College occupied the east end of the new building, a private collegiate space beyond the rood-screen, but at eventide, when the scholars were occupied elsewhere, choristers, clerks and chaplains would process into the vast, empty, candlelit space of the church itself to sing Vespers and Compline before a gilded statue of the Blessed Virgin or beneath the painting of the Assumption of the Virgin (no longer extant, alas) on the south wall. There in the candlelight our visitor might observe the choir, sixteen or so in number, grouped around a grand book on a solid, handsomely appointed lectern. A scholar of our own time has imagined the scene:

Opened up, the book is vast in every respect, more than two feet tall, over three feet from side to side, a thick weight of fine parchment pages. Its contents, too, are impressively large. Words and music stand out in bold calligraphy, easy to read even from a distance of several feet. Black ink and red ink alternate in a glorious medley. Fine capital letters, vividly coloured, add to the air of luxury. Boys in their teens are at the front, peering up to the tops of the pages where their music is written. Around them stand the men. One of them beats time, directing the performance. Another turns the book's pages, each time sending the candles into a frenzy. All eyes are on the page, for the light is fickle, the music unpredictable, and a moment's error will place the whole performance in jeopardy.[4]

Since most of the music in the Eton Choirbook cannot be sung at all unless it is sung supremely well, we can be certain that the original choristers were both gifted and exceptionally well trained. The basis of the training was plainchant, music

4 John Milsom, *The Voices of Angels, Music from the Eton Choirbook*, Vol. V, Collins Classics, 1995, C D booklet note p. 4.

that demands absolute pitch and faultless unison, to which was added the acquisition of flawless breath-control and a coloratura-like agility in the high-lying tessitura. The choristers would also be taught to improvise complex vocal counterpoints, a basic skill which helped turn them into competent composers in their own right.

Eton's first named composer of distinction is Walter Lambe, admitted to the College as a King's scholar on 8 July, 1467. Lambe would have studied the work of his elders in the choir, imagining ways of improving on their music-making by the introduction of new vocal combinations and new, mathematically elaborate groundplans.[5] It is possible to imagine our visitor to Eton *c.* 1500 hearing Lambe's sublime short Marian antiphon 'Nesciens mater' sung in the intimate space of the church's collegiate choir. It is a piece in which the words are every bit as sensual as the music itself:

Unknowing, a Virgin Mother gave birth without pain to a man who was to be Saviour of the Ages. A virgin alone gave milk, her breasts filled from heaven, to none other than the King of Angels.[6]

On a Feast Day or at Vespers, he might hear Lambe's altogether grander 'Salve Regina'. Earthbound, the music soars aloft; unmoving, it moves in time; chaste, it ravishes sense. If he is an experienced listener, he will be familiar with the choral forces and their allotted roles: the sumptuous-sounding choral euphony of the lower and middle voices, the tenors' *cantus firmus* anchoring proceedings, the trebles' spiralling descants. He will also know that he must eventually surrender

5 A more 'developed' antiphon might have the 2nd and 4th verses in triple time, the 6th and 8th verses in duple or quadruple time, and the 10th and 12th verses again in triple time, with interesting textural changes linking, say, the 4th and 8th verses.

6 Nesciens Mater virgo virum peperit sine dolore salvatorem saeculorum. Ipsum regem angelorum sola virgo lactabat ubera de caelo plena.

8

thought to feeling, much as we do nowadays when the Marschallin, a latter-day Madonna, leads us entranced into the tendril-like beauties of the Trio of the final act of Richard Strauss's *Der Rosenkavalier*.[7]

As the prescription for the College's coat-of-arms made clear, there was to be nothing half-hearted about Eton's Mariolatry. The hope is expressed that the 'three flowers of lilies argent on a field of sable' might

bring forth the brightest flowers redolent in every kind of science to the honour and most devout worship of Almighty God and of the undefiled Virgin and glorious Mother, to whom as in other things, and most especially in this our foundation, we offer *with burning mind hearty and most vehement devotion* [my emphasis].

In this late-fifteenth-century scheme of things, even the Trinity could be upstaged. In Richard Davy's glorious 'O domine caeli terraeque creator' what is ostensibly a celebration of the Trinity rapidly becomes a prayer to the Blessed Virgin, the trebles' entry, at the words 'Mariam Deo dignissimam', lofty, tender, and sweet.

The most important of many festivals in the Eton calendar was the Virgin's own festival, the Feast of the Assumption on 15 August. This inspired Wylkynson's masterpiece, a nine-part setting of 'Salve Regina'. Based on the plainchant antiphon 'Assumpta est Maria in caelis', and almost certainly designed to be sung before the illustration of the Annunciation on the

7 Compare Wilfrid Mellers's comments on William Cornysh's setting of the *Magnificat*: 'Although the singing parts wing in ec-stasis, their textures remaining prevailingly consonant, making little attempt to 'express', let alone 'illustrate', words. We wouldn't expect God to fuss overmuch about our follies and foibles; endeavouring to invent what may pass as His music, we opt for grace, light and concord: out of which may be typically generated a rapture that seems, momentarily, to be 'out of this world' and its vale of tears.'

south wall of the Eton church, it recreates in music an image of Mary being received into heaven surrounded by the angelic host. The Choirbook actually labels the voice-parts in descending order of rank with illustrations of Seraphs, Cherubs, Thrones, Dominations, Virtues, Powers, Principalities, Archangels and Angels.

Another piece by Wylkynson borders on the bizarre. It is his thirteen-part setting of the Apostles' Creed. Since there was no immediate use for this within the Eton choral liturgy, it was probably written for performance by choristers and scholars as a musical complement to the rood-screen which is thought to have been decorated with images of the twelve apostles. With the text divided into twelve segments and a thirteenth line (a plainsong fragment, 'Jesus autem transiens', 'Jesus walked among them') added by way of preface and postlude, the creed is sung as a thirteen-part round, the first voice moving onto the second segment as the second voice intones the first, and so on. Even though the music is harmonically static, there is a serious risk here of a rapid descent into cacophony, the more so if partly trained singers are being deployed. Visually, though, the piece would have been spectacular: the thirteen soloists ranged before the rood-screen or across the altar steps in symbolic representation of Christ and his apostles.

Though there were originally nine pieces by Wylkynson in the Eton Choirbook, twelve by Lambe, and fifteen by John Browne, whose 'O Maria Salvatoris Mater' stands at the head of the anthology and who may have had Eton connections, the vast majority of the music was collected and edited from non-Etonian sources. A 'Magnificat' by the Canterbury-based composer John Nesbett, which can also be found in a contemporary Scottish manuscript source, is typical of the far-flung nature of the anthology. The limitations of the Eton book are the lost folios (the surviving volume contains 126 of the 224 leaves listed in the index) and the absence of settings of the Mass.[8] Of the losses, the most regrettable from the historical point of view is the five-part setting of 'Gaude flore virginali' by Dunstable himself.

Easter provided the climax to the liturgical year. Scholars as well as choristers attended Matins and Vespers throughout Lent and Holy Week as well as being involved in a lengthy roster of secular activities and liturgical rites. The Eton Choirbook's most notable Easter piece is Davy's *St Matthew Passion*, the oldest extant polyphonic setting of the Passion story by a named composer. In earlier times, the story had been intoned by deacons playing the roles of the Evangelist, Christ, and the turba (the crowd and the various ancillary characters). In Davy's setting, the use of polyphony transforms the crowd scenes both musically and dramatically. The impact on the scholars and fellows seated in the chancel on Palm Sunday must have been considerable.

There is drama of a different kind in settings by Davy, Browne and William Cornysh of the anonymous thirteenth-century Good Friday poem *Stabat mater dolorosa*. The poem, which exists in a number of versions, offers the composer an awkward mix of high drama and low doggerel. (When Rossini set it three centuries later, his initial instinct was to farm out the doggerel to an assistant.) All three settings are touched by genius in the climactic stanza

8 There were 93 works in the Choirbook. 43 survive complete in the rebound edition, 21 are incomplete, and 29 are lost. Masses at Eton may have been said or, if sung, not sung polyphonically.

Et dum stetit generosa dolorosa,
Plebs tunc canit clamorosa:
'Crucifige! Crucifige!'

The Browne and Cornysh settings have been more written about but it is the Davy which offers us an almost Bach-like directness of utterance.

We should not be surprised to discover in the Choirbook music which mimics contemporary painting and literature in its complex layering of meaning. The most striking example is Browne's 'Stabat iuxta Christi crucem' which combines a variation of the traditional 'Stabat mater' text with Edmund Turges's partsong 'From stormy wyndis and grevous wethir / Good Lord, preserve the Estridge Feather'. The original partsong had called on the Blessed Virgin to protect Prince Arthur, Henry VII's eldest son, on a forthcoming journey. In Browne's antiphon, which was written after Arthur's death in 1502, the journey is that of Arthur's soul to heaven. The grieving mother becomes both the Blessed Virgin and Arthur's mother, Queen Elizabeth.

The most advanced music in the Choirbook is by Cornysh, who died in 1523. Much of his work is consonant with other pieces in the collection, though if we examine his 'Salve Regina', with its astonishing use of dissonance in the dramatisation of what is by now a tiresomely familiar text (there are 66 rival settings in the Choirbook), we are left with a sense of being on the brink of another era altogether.

*

The Choirbook and its repertory escaped the worst vicissitudes of Henry VIII's Reformation. Henry's argument was with Rome, not with the Catholic faith to which he remained unswervingly loyal, or with the musicians who served it. For its part, Eton no doubt learned to modify its Mariolatry.

What Eton could not avoid, however, was the chaos which followed Henry's death and the drive by the new Protestant ascendancy to root out all trace of medieval Catholicism. Unlike many charitable foundations, Eton did not have its assets confiscated, nor was its church ransacked by reformist parishioners as was the case elsewhere in the kingdom. Edward VI's Protectorship did impose on Eton a new Provost but its candidate, the 34-year-old Dr Thomas Smith, was no fanatic. An expert on the Tudor constitution and, under Elizabeth I, a diplomat and privy councillor, he attended to the Protestantization of Eton with civility and care. The church was inevitably divested of much of its ornamentation and the Marian frescoes were whitewashed over. The college was also searched for 'superstitious' books. However, the Choirbook itself was either overlooked – or left undisturbed in its trunk in the organ-loft on the grounds that it was an elegantly produced but no longer dangerous artefact. If any of its music was still being used, which is unlikely, it would have had to be abandoned in compliance with the edict of 1547 which banned the use of all anthems except 'those of Our Lord and they in English, set to a plain and distinct note for every syllable'. Music itself was not proscribed – the College continued to acquire wind and string instruments for the use of boys and masters – but a break in the employment of the Master of the Choristers, William Butler, between 1550 and January 1555 suggests the imposition of a radically changed regime where the choristers were concerned.

After the death of Edward VI in 1553 and the ascent to the throne of the Catholic Queen Mary, the pendulum swung violently the other way. Even before Provost Smith's resignation in July 1554, the Eton church had been partly restored to its former state. The two organs were overhauled by John Howe, the son of the man who had supplied them in 1506-8 for the sum of £5. 13s. 4d. New bells, chalices and altar-cloths were acquired. The holy-water stoup was returned to its place by the door.

We do not know precisely when the Choirbook was taken to London to be rebound. 1553-4 is the most probable date. Why it was decided to have it rebound is also something of a mystery. The most likely explanation is that Eton was hoping either to revive the repertory or use some of the music to tide the choir over until new repertory was created. It is equally conceivable that the book was simply being rebound as a valued art-work, a Catholic icon. Whatever the explanation, sending it to London would have been a risky undertaking. Had it fallen into the wrong hands, it might well have ended up as binders' waste or worse.

If the rebound Choirbook already had limited practical use by the time of its return to Eton, Mary's death in 1558 finally rendered it redundant. Under the Elizabethan settlement, Eton ceased to be a Catholic seminary and became what it has remained ever since, an Anglican school with a continuous and intermittently distinguished musical tradition.

The Choirbook was not entirely forgotten. Some time between 1581 and 1606, the celebrated anthologist John Baldwin, a lay clerk at St George's, Windsor, copied Wylkynson's 13-part setting of the Apostles' Creed into his Commonplace Book. Items were also copied by two distinguished eighteenth-century musicians and antiquarians, Henry Needler and John Travers. After that, little is heard of it until the early 1880s when two Collegers, M. R. James and Henry Babington Smith, managed, as James later recalled, to 'wheedle the keys of the Fellows' Library out of Vice-Provost Dupuis' and 'unearth from the dusty top shelf the huge Anthem Book of the early years of the sixteenth century, written for Eton Chapel'.

It was a happy survival. Had the Eton Choirbook vanished as others did, a gap would exist in the annals of English music comparable to the loss of the anthems of Purcell or the finest works of the early nineteenth-century Anglican choral revival.

The Bells

The single bell which nowadays announces that a service is about to begin in College Chapel still inspires the occasional letter of complaint to the *Eton College Chronicle* from Sunday-morning lie-abeds. They should take comfort from the fact that it was worse in the old days. Eton's earliest benefactors – the kings, princes and well-to-do families who gave handsome endowments in return for the saying in perpetuity of masses for the repose of their souls – were exceptionally keen on bells.

When Edward IV's father-in-law, Earl Rivers, secured for Eton a royal grant of property in the City of London, the Provost and Fellows bound themselves and their successors to 'cause a masse dayly to be seid within the Churche of the seid College, at the auter of our lady' at 7.15 each morning. It was further provided that sixty [*sic*] 'knolles or strokes' should daily be sounded 'with a grete belle in the seid College nye afore the beginnying of the seide masse, so that wel disposed people may have knowledge to come to the seide mass'.

One of the many unrealised items in Henry VI's grandiose revision of his plans for Eton's minster church was a bell tower adjacent to the Slough Road. This would have been as high as the tower of Magdalen College, Oxford, with room for a peal of up to ten bells. At some stage after the demolition of the old parish church, a rather more modest wooden campanile, hung with five bells, was erected in the churchyard. It was later dismantled by the Puritans and though the bells themselves were retrieved and stored in the chapel, they were eventually sold for scrap in the 1770s.

Other bells took their place. As Henry Salt, the Victorian chronicler, would recall in *Memories of Bygone Eton*:

Silver bells, golden bells, brazen bells, and iron bells, but also, and most significant, chapel bells… there is no sound that bides more steadfastly in the mind of an Etonian than that rather harsh, persistent signal, familiar to every member of the school, like a voice which, without being unduly raised, conveyed an imperious summons which none could ignore.

In Salt's day, the bells were often associated with rural escapades:

Once with two or three school-fellows, I walked, or ran, to Burnham Beeches on a Sunday afternoon, an excursion which it was just, and only just, possible to make between the hours of dinner and chapel. The pitiless bells began while we were still on our return, some distance from Eton, in the field beyond the Slough road; and I have never forgotten the breathless anxiety of our final rush, which just brought us to the chapel as the Provost and Headmaster, preceded by the Sixth Form, were making their pompous entry.

Nowadays, the bell's toll is complemented by the sweet-sounding chime of the clock on Lupton's Tower and the roar of aircraft overhead. The latter, one assumes, is tolerated by our Sunday-morning lie-abed. Aircraft noise does not stir the conscience, bells do.

CHAPTER 2

Commonwealth and Restoration

Eton did not immediately shed its reputation as a choir school of distinction. Sir Henry Savile, who was Provost from 1596 to 1622, may have loathed wits ('If I would look for Witts I would goe to Newgate, there be Witts') but he was determined that Eton should be as learned a society as any in Europe.

In 1613, the College placed an order for a new organ with the distinguished organ-builder, Thomas Dallam. A new organ-loft was commissioned, local craftsmen were brought in to build and paint the case ('*item* gelting, painting and vernishinge £10. os. od'), and an experienced organist, the 50-year-old composer and choirmaster Leonard Woodson, was lured away from St George's Chapel, Windsor. With a new organ, ten choristers, and nine clerks at his disposal, Woodson had ample resources with which to run an expert specialist choir.

Eton survived the Civil War and Commonwealth relatively unscathed under the stern but benign rule of its Puritan Provost, Francis Rous. There was, inevitably, radical reform of the college's religious life. College Church, which was now treated as a large parish church, became College Chapel, Chaplains became Conducts ('conductitti et remoti', 'hireable and fireable'), and the building was stripped of 'all scandalous monuments and pictures'. Surplices were outlawed as an offence against 'law and the liberty of the subject' and the choral contribution reduced to a diet of psalms.

As the number of choristers was systematically reduced, so the singing men looked for work elsewhere, initially in Windsor, then, when the St George's Choir was disbanded by the Puritans, further afield. An Eton Fellow, Thomas Weaver, resolved to keep music alive by arranging musical events for the redundant choristers but he was a man who was constantly falling foul of authority. Though he had done much to beautify College Chapel in the 1630s, he had been accused by Archbishop Laud of shortening morning prayer on a holy day so as to have more time 'to pull down a tree' and 'making a sawpit in the churchyard'. Now he found himself being confronted by the new Governor of Windsor, the regicide-in-waiting, Colonel John Venn. Weaver's reply to the charge of favouring 'popish music' above the psalms – 'God is as well pleased with being served in tune as out of tune' – is quoted in all the histories. What is not reported is Venn's reaction.

Because it was a school, not a cathedral or chapel royal, Eton did not lose its choir entirely. Indeed, during the 1650s, it added to its strength thanks to the wheeler-dealing of one of Eton's most enigmatic figures, the music-loving Puritan divine, Nathaniel Ingelo, who became a Fellow in 1650 at the age of 29. In 1653, Ingelo took into his and Eton's employ the Windsor-born organist and composer, Benjamin Rogers. It was a somewhat irregular appointment, not least because Rogers lacked a degree, an omission Ingelo rectified by requesting Cromwell to instruct the University of Cambridge to provide him with one.

The poet Andrew Marvell, who was living in Eton as private tutor to Cromwell's ward, William Dutton, and who was himself looking to seek political advancement through Ingelo's good offices, appears to have taken an amused interest in these musical machinations. Towards the end of his Latin poem 'A Letter to Doctor Ingelo (Then with my Lord Whitlocke, Ambassador, from the Protector to the Queen of Sweden)' he addresses Ingelo:

> Nos sine te frustra Thamisis saliceta subimus,
> Sparsaque per steriles turba vagamur agros.
> Et male tentanti querulum respondet avena:
> Quin et Rogerio dissiluere fides.[1]

Rogers was organist at Eton from 1661-4, when he moved to Magdalen College, Oxford where he remained until he was dismissed, aged 73, for 'noisy talk in the organ-loft' and his refusal to play services 'as they were willing and able to sing, but out of a thwarting humour would play nothing but the Canterbury tune'. The Victorians were extremely fond of *Rogers in D* but he is nowadays chiefly remembered for his setting of the college grace which forms the basis of the music sung each May Day morning from the top of Magdalen College tower.

Historians have routinely claimed that there was precious little musical activity in Eton in the seventeenth, eighteenth and early nineteenth centuries. This is difficult to credit given the presence within Eton during these years of a succession of distinguished musicians – organists, choirmasters, musical copyists – whose very existence must have touched the life of the community in one way or another. Towards the end of the seventeenth century, Eton had significant connections with three of the country's most distinguished composers, Pelham

---

1 Without you, we go in vain under the willows of the Thames / A scattered band, we wander through barren fields, / And the pipe responds mournfully to those attempting it unskilfully. / And, indeed, Rogers' strings have burst asunder.

Humfrey, John Blow, and Henry Purcell. A primary source for the music of Humfrey and Blow is the vast collection of Restoration church music assembled by Bartholomew Isaak, a singing man at Eton from 1673 until his death in 1703.

Isaak's younger colleague, John Walter, who was organist and choirmaster from 1681 to 1704, had even closer connections. A pupil of Blow, he almost certainly assisted at the first performance of Blow's delightful court masque *Venus and Adonis* in 1683. Among those who benefited from Walter's care at Eton – and from Eton's own generosity long before multimillion pound scholarship funds were set in place – was John Weldon, a Purcell *protégé* who would later hold important positions with the Chapel Royal and the church of St Martin-in-the-Fields. Eton's accounts for December 1693 show '£5 towards putting out Weldon the chorister for half a year'. Later we find 'Paid for Weldon to Mr H. Purcell £1. 10s' and again 'Allowed by the College to Mr H. Purcell with Weldon the chorister for half a year ended at Lady Day 1694 £5'.

*

The relationship with St George's, Windsor, which had flourished informally during Cromwell's time, became closer still during the years following the Restoration, to Eton's future disadvantage. There were pressing practical reasons for these arrangements. The shortage of trained church musicians in the aftermath of the Puritan interregnum was one; another was Eton's parlous financial state in the 1670s. The Provost and Fellows must have agreed to the strategy, despite its being a flagrant breach of Henry VI's statute barring Eton's choristers and clerks from singing with the St George's choir.

Eton did, however, retain a number of boy choristers and towards the end of the century money was lavished on College Chapel as part of the renovation and beautification of Eton which took place during Henry Godolphin's time as Provost. In addition to a new roof and elaborate wood panelling in the style of the period, the chapel was provided with a handsome new Bernard ('Father') Smith organ (£789. 2s. 6d.) and a new and somewhat inappropriate plinth on which to place it. It must have looked decidedly odd: a Greek portico, its 25-foot-deep entablature resting on fluted Doric columns, approached by a small flight of steps a third of the way down a medieval English church newly refurbished after the manner of a Caroline country gentleman's best parlour.

At some point during the Restoration period, Choral Matins had been dispensed with but Evensong was retained. The repertory available for this is documented in the College organ books of the period, music copied for use at Eton by Isaak, Walter, and their successor Benjamin Lamb. In addition to anthems and services by Tallis, Byrd, and Gibbons, there is music by most of the leading church composers of the day: Child, Rogers, Humfrey, Blow, Purcell, Goldwin, and Croft.

Lamb was eventually succeeded by John Pigott, who took formal control of both choirs in 1733. For the best part of a century and a half, Eton chapel now danced more or less exclusively to Windsor's tune, until, in 1867, the Dean and Chapter of St George's ordered the separation of the two choirs with effect from Christmas that year.

CHAPTER 3

Dr Thomas Arne

Thomas Augustine Arne (1710-88) was not Eton's first composer of distinction, Walter Lambe preceded him by two centuries, but the belief that he was has caused him to be accorded a peculiar place of honour in Eton's musical pantheon.

The Arnes were a colourful crew. Arne's father was a well-known upholsterer and funeral director in King Street, Covent Garden who would do anything to make money. Providing a private billet for North American Indian chiefs was one ruse; pirating Handel's *Acis and Galatea* as part of a fledgling season of English opera at the New Theatre, Haymarket was another. Thomas's grandfather died in debt in the Marshalsea Prison and his uncle Edward ended up in the Fleet Prison. Thomas was fifteen when:

By an accident on a Sunday, the door being opened, [Edward] ran into the parlour adjoining the [prison] chapel during the time of Divine Service: he had no covering for his body but the feathers of a bed into which he had crept to defend himself from the cold, and the feathers stuck and were clotted upon him by his own excrement and the dirt which covered his skin.

Sending Thomas to Eton was a calculated ploy. It was hoped that by advancing himself academically and mingling with the well-to-do he would lay the foundations for a successful career in the law – a well-heeled lawyer being the one in-house service the Arnes manifestly lacked. Sadly for them, it was not to be. As Arne's pupil, the revered musical chronicler Dr Charles Burney, would later recall:

Arne had a good school education, having been sent to Eton by his father, who intended him for the law. But I have been assured by several of his schoolfellows, that his love of music operated on him too powerfully, even when he was at Eton, for his own peace or that of his companions; for with a miserable cracked common-flute, he used to torment them night and day, when not obliged to attend school.

In this respect, Eton must have been preferable to home, where Arne claimed that hostility to his music-making obliged him to practise either at night (muffling the sound of his spinet with a handkerchief) or away from the house altogether. His violin teacher, Michael Festing, one of London's finest fiddle-players, is said to have found Arne practising in his father's funeral parlour using a coffin as an improvised music-stand. Festing expressed relief that there was no corpse in the coffin, at which point Arne opened the lid to prove otherwise.

According to Burney, Arne's father eventually realised that his son was spending more time on music than on his legal studies. Calling at the house of a gentleman of quality, he discovered a concert in progress in which his son was performing:

Finding him more admired for his musical talents than knowledge in the law, he was soon prevailed upon to forgive his unruly passion, and to let him try to turn it to some account. No sooner was the young man able to practise aloud in his father's house, than he bewitched the whole family.

This sounds too good to be true: the sentimental end to some minor Restoration comedy. That said, Arne did become a musician. His family had to look elsewhere for their legal advice.

The Arnes were Catholics. This had not affected Thomas's attending Eton but it did mean that he was unlikely to find work at court or within the Anglican Church. This was no great deprivation. Arne was first and foremost a pleasure-seeking man of the theatre, an expert on the female voice (and other female attributes), and a gifted song-writer who in the middle years of the century managed to corner the market as composer-in-chief at the Vauxhall pleasure gardens.

Staid opinion thought him sleazy and arrogant. Dr Burney's daughter, the novelist Fanny Burney, did not pull her punches where Arne was concerned:

Thoughtless, dissipated, and careless, he neglected or rather scoffed at all other but musical reputation. And he was so little scrupulous in his idea of propriety, that he took pride, rather than shame, in being publicly charged, even in the decline of life, as a man of pleasure. Such a character was ill qualified to form or protect the morals of a youthful pupil, and it is probable that not a notion of duty ever occurred to Dr Arne, so happy was his self-complacency in the fertility of his invention and the ease of his compositions, and so dazzled by the brilliancy of his success in his powers of melody – which, in truth, for the English stage were in sweetness and variety unrivalled – that, satisfied and flattered by the practical exertions and the popularity of his fancy, he had no ambition, or rather, no thought concerning the theory of his art.

It is difficult to disagree with much of this. Arne was arguably the most talented English-born composer of his generation (his exquisite sunrise-and-lark-filled cantata *The Morning* would not seem out of place in Handel's *L'Allegro ed il Penseroso* or Haydn's *The Seasons*) yet it was a talent he chose to exploit rather than develop. At the age of 27, he thought himself up to turning Milton's *Comus* into a three-act masque (Covent Garden, 1738). In the event, the piece trades charm for moral uplift, salaciousness for evil.

These, though, were the very qualities which made Arne's Vauxhall Gardens offerings so effective. No one knew better than he how to deploy suspensions and sweet-sounding appoggiaturas in a way guaranteed to bring a tear to the eye of even the most bibulous womaniser. On home ground, in rakish man-about-town mode in something like his cantata *Frolic and be Free*, Arne was incomparable. Only he, among English composers of the time, would have contemplated using a sensuous minuet as the backdrop to the contemplation of a night of slow, untroubled love-making.

It was during his time at the Vauxhall Gardens that Arne cornered the market in Shakespeare song settings, creating a style which would last well into the twentieth century. The best of these settings sound like genuine folk-songs, new-gathered with the dew fresh upon them. They were no such thing, of course. Arne's 'Where the Bee sucks, there lurk I' is a small bespoke jewel, an exquisitely crafted art-song whose brevity and evanescence is perfectly calculated to leave audiences craving more. These Shakespeare settings would probably have secured Arne a place in the national consciousness, even without the help of 'God Save the King', which he arranged and popularised, and 'Rule Britannia!' which he wrote as the denouement for his *The Masque of Alfred*.

*

The Masque of Alfred had its premiere at Cliveden in Berkshire on 1 August, 1740. Spectacularly situated high above the River Thames three miles upstream from Maidenhead, Cliveden was the home of Frederick Prince of Wales (1707-51). At loggerheads with his father, George II, and his father's Prime Minister, Sir Robert Walpole, Frederick had leased the house from the Countess of Orkney in 1737 with the explicit aim of setting up a court-in-waiting. Music was a particular passion (racing, cards, cricket, and drinking were others) though even here Frederick sought to snub his Handel-loving father by cultivating rival musicians not heard at court. In this, as in other matters, Arne was his man.

The text of *The Masque of Alfred* is by two Scottish-born writers James Thomson and David Mallet, assisted by their patron, Prince Frederick's secretary, Eton-educated George Lyttelton. Lyttelton's involvement is a clear indication that the piece was intended to have a political dimension. In the masque, Alfred is characterised as the consensual ruler-in-waiting of a patriotic people threatened from without. Issues such as these were much discussed by Lyttelton's cousin, Viscount Cobham, a veteran of Marlborough's army, whose so-called 'Boy Patriots'[1] met regularly in the Temple of Friendship which he had erected in his gardens at Stowe in honour of Frederick's visit there in 1737.

Arne's music for *The Masque of Alfred* shows him at his best, expert and effective with moments of imaginative daring

---

[1] The 'Boy Patriots' included Cobham's young nephews the Grenvilles, George Lyttelton, and William Pitt. In his *A History of England* (London, 1950), Keith Feiling describes Cobham and his *protégés* as 'Firmly Whig and Protestant... ambitious and high-minded, jealous for themselves and for British good fame, contemptuous of Hanover and foes to corruption'.

which hint at something altogether finer. (The Spirit's brief declamatory Air 'Hear, Alfred, hear, father of the state' has a vocal and instrumental eloquence worthy of Gluck.) The setting of the concluding number, 'The celebrated ode in honour of Great Britain call'd Rule Britannia' (Thomson's work, in all probability), is a *tour de force*. It was Wagner who remarked that the first ten notes of the refrain encapsulate to perfection the English character.

The Masque of Alfred was revived in expanded form in London in March 1745. With the Jacobite threat at its most intense, 'Rule Britannia' and 'God Save the King' which Arne arranged that autumn, won positions for themselves in national life which they have retained ever since.

They also set a precedent. Since that time, Etonians have had a hand in the writing of each of England's principal anthems. Arne wrote the music for 'God Save the King' and 'Rule Britannia', Parry set Blake's 'Jerusalem', A. C. Benson wrote the words for 'Land of Hope and Glory', Cecil Spring-Rice wrote the words of the hymn 'I vow to thee my country'.

*

Not all Arne's works were successes. His opera *The Guardian Outwitted* closed within a week of its opening at Covent Garden in December 1764, a failure which inspired the anonymously published *An Elegy on the death of THE GUARDIAN OUTWITTED, an opera written and composed by T. A. Arne* in which a parody of Gray's *Elegy* is used to lampoon Arne and his opera. The handsomely produced quarto volume has the original at the foot of each page:

> Can storied urn, or animated bust,
> Back to its mansion call the fleeting breath?
> Can honour's voice provoke the silent dust,
> Or flattery soothe the dull cold ear of death?

and the parody above it:

> Can pensive ARNE, with animated Strain,
> Back to its Audience call his fleeting Play?
> Can Music's Voice the Hand of death restrain,
> Or soothing Sounds prolong the fatal Day?

Two Etonians pilloried for the price of one.

Thomas Gray

Thomas Gray had many interests – literary, musical, antiquarian, botanical, topographical – and an affectionate, informal, often idiosyncratic way of writing about them. Opera was a particular passion. Shortly after leaving Eton in 1734, he attended a performance of Purcell's *King Arthur* at a fashionable new theatre in Goodman's Fields in the City of London:

The second scene is a British temple, enough to make one go back a thousand years and really be in ancient Britain: the songs are all Church-musick, & in every one of the choruses Mrs Chambers sung the chief part, accompanied with Roarings, Squawlings & Squeakations dire.[1]

Gray had been at Eton at the fag-end of Benjamin Lamb's time as organist and choirmaster; 'Church musick' was not a term of approbation where Gray was concerned.

Travels in Italy, which Gray first visited at the age of 23 in 1739, confirmed his passion for opera. To Anglo-Saxon taste, it was the most disreputable of musical forms, which is precisely what Gray loved about it: the noise, the spectacle, and the sense of danger afforded by Italian theatres where aficionados rubbed shoulders with gamblers, whores and drunken soldiery. When English audiences took to behaving in a similar way, Gray was delighted. 'I have known candles lighted, broken bottles, & penknives flung on the stage, the

---

1 '*Gorgons* and *Hydra's*, and *Chimera's* dire', John Milton, *Paradise Lost*, ii, 628

benches torn up, the scenes hurried into the street & set on fire,' he told the Italian author Count Francesco Algarotti in a letter in 1763. The opera was Mancini's *Gl'amanti generosi* (Naples, 1705). His letter went on:

There was one girl (she call'd herself the Niccolina) with little voice & less beauty; but with the utmost justness of ear, the strongest expression of countenance, the most speaking eyes, the greatest vivacity & variety of gesture. Her first appearance instantly fix'd their attention, the tumult sank at once, or if any murmur rose, it was soon hush'd by a general cry for silence. Her first air ravish'd every body; they forgot their prejudices, they forgot that they did not understand a word of the language; they enter'd into all the humour of the part, made her repeat all her songs, & continued their transports, their laughter, & applause to the end of the piece.

Gray had no illusions about the fragility of the English love-affair with opera:

The truth is, the opera itself, tho' supported here at great expense for so many years, has rather maintained itself by the admiration bestow'd on a few particular voices, or the borrow'd taste of a few men of condition, that have learn'd in Italy how to admire, than by any genuine love we bear to the best Italian musick.

As to the lack of a flourishing home-grown English operatic tradition, he blamed the English language

... which in spite of its energy, plenty, & the crowd of excellent writers this nation has produced, does yet (I am sorry to say it) retain too much of its barbarous original to adapt itself to musical composition. I by no means wish to have been born any thing but an Englishman; yet I should rejoice to exchange tongues with Italy.

One particular piece of musical exotica which caught Gray's attention was the new and newly fashionable glass harmonica. In a letter dated 28 March, 1760, he observed: 'No instrument that I know, has so celestial a tone. I thought it was a Cherubim in a box.'

Like all the best writers on music, Gray had the language at his disposal to make the experience vivid.

CHAPTER 4

Eton's Handelians

The Revd Thomas Morell, Lord Sandwich, Joah Bates

A celebrated bout of fisticuffs in School Yard is the principal reason why Thomas Morell (1703-84) has featured in histories of Eton down the years. In fact, he was a figure of some consequence in musical and church circles in eighteenth century England. A King's Scholar, born and brought up in Eton, he was Handel's principal librettist in his later years and an interested chronicler of the composer's working methods.

The fisticuffs were the result an academic disputation between Morell and fellow Colleger William Battie which had continued beyond the formal confines of Upper School. As Morell would later recall: 'After a fair set-to, I knocked his head against the Chapel wall and this put an end to the affair for the present'. 'For the present' is the operative phrase. To the fury of Morell's mother (a saddler's wife and an Eton Dame), Battie's mother (the widow of an Eton master) turned up in College and delivered 'a swinging slap on the face' to the 'aggressor' Morell.

Morell was a classicist destined for the church. His several editions of Greek tragedies were prepared with Eton boys in mind, as was his elaborately titled and possibly less widely appreciated *Sacred Annals, or the Life of Christ, as recorded by the Four Evangelists, with Particular Observations designed for General Use but particularly for the Sunday Exercise of the Young Gentlemen educated at Eton College*. He also had a passion for music, which Eton appears to have encouraged (he was an organist of sorts) and an interest in wide swathes of English literature back to Chaucer whose works he translated.

After winning a fellowship at King's College, Cambridge, Morell was presented with a college living at Buckland in Hertfordshire, though since he was much in demand as a preacher, scholar, wit and socialite, he was rarely resident there. In his *Literary Anecdotes of the Eighteenth Century*, John Nicholls would recall:

> He was warm in his attachments; and was a cheerful and entertaining companion. He loved a jest, told a good story, was fond of musick, and would occasionally indulge his friends with a song. In his exterior appearance, however, he never condescended to study the Graces; and, unfortunately for himself, he was a total stranger to oeconomy.

Morell first offered his services to Handel in 1745. Like Arne, he was a member of Prince of Wales's Cliveden set, enabling him to bolster his approach with 'the honour of a recommendation from Prince Frederick'. The offer was timely. With the Jacobite Rising causing panic in government and a certain bellicose, backs-to-the-wall patriotism in the country at large, Handel was called upon in his capacity as expensively retained court composer to stir the nation's soul. He produced two works in 1745-6, his *Occasional Oratorio*, for which its is widely believed Morell assembled the texts, and *Judas Maccabaeus* whose libretto is certainly by Morell.

Morell was better equipped than we might suppose for the task of libretto-writing. Eighteenth century librettists were generally minor men of letters capable of transcribing and versifying a story – usually, in Handel's case, from an Old Testament source – and glossing it with the religious and political ideas of the day. Nationhood was one such idea; the rebuttal of the Deists was another. To the Deists, for whom God was the creator of the world but not its all-determining intelligence, the Old Testament Jews were a deracinated group of ex-slaves, savage war-mongers, factious, conceited and unstable. To the Anglican Morell, the position was quite other. As God's children, the Israelites are seen as gentlemen-warriors boldly and successfully confronting the godless aggressor.

Morell was no dramatist but he was well versed in classical theatre and was sufficiently acquainted with the work of Handel's earlier librettists to think himself capable of serving what he called this 'impatient, peremptory, exacting' man. Libretto-writing, he later wrote with lordly insouciance, is journeyman's work 'especially if it be considered what alterations [the librettist] must submit to, if the Composer be of an haughty disposition, and has but an imperfect acquaintance with the English language'.

The first act of *Judas Maccabaeus* was sketched within a week of Morell receiving the commission. He delivered it in person to Handel at his house in London's Brook Street and would later recall the following exchange:

HANDEL Well, and how are you to go on?
MORELL Why, we are to suppose an engagement, and that the Israelites have conquered, and so begin with a chorus as 'Fallen is the Foe' or, something like it.
HANDEL No, I will have this. *Begins working it upon the harpsichord.* Well, go on.
MORELL I will bring you more tomorrow.
HANDEL No, something now!
MORELL 'So fall thy Foes, O Lord...'
HANDEL That will do. *Continues working at the harpsichord.*

Morell's verses are rarely well 'finished'. Strings of sibilants and awkward consonant clusters abound. Did he have a poor 'ear' or did this early glimpse of Handel at work convince him that there was simply no need to polish and refine?

In the summer of 1747, Morell worked with Handel on his Alexander-and-Cleopatra oratorio *Alexander Balus* whose third act begins with what Morell describes as 'an incomparable Air in the *affetuoso* style, intermixed with the chorus recitative which follows it'. When Morell first brought his verses to Handel all was not well:

HANDEL Damn your Iambics!

MORELL Don't put yourself in a passion, they are easily Trochees.

HANDEL Trochees! What are Trochees?

MORELL Why, the very reverse of Iambics, by leaving out a syllable in every line, as instead of 'Convey me to some peaceful shore' [we have] 'Lead me to some peaceful shore'.

HANDEL That is what I want.

MORELL I will step into the parlour, and alter them immediately.

When Morell returned with the promised trochees three minutes later, he found that Handel had already set the iambs as a memorable air, desolate and resigned, 'accompanied with only a quaver, and a rest of 3 quavers'.

Morell's work with Handel won him prestige in both musical and ecclesiastical circles; so much so, that in 1746 he was invited to deliver a sermon in Worcester Cathedral during the Three Choirs Festival. His subject was an imposing one: 'The Use and Importance of Music in the Sacrifice of Thanksgiving'. The text, which was published the following year, is laden with high-flown blather – 'O Harmony! sacred Harmony! Saints, the greatest Saints upon Earth have enjoy'd thee in rational Pleasure' – but is often shrewd on the subject in question:

Seeing, then, that Music seizeth irresistibly upon the Affections, and, when duly attended to, can raise and still govern the Passions, with an almost arbitrary Sway; who can doubt the Utility of it in religious Worship?... Let the united Force of [the organ] strike up an Alarm; how swiftly *do the straggling Thoughts return to Duty* [Morell's emphasis]?

Morell uses the address to expatiate on music's innate majesty and significance:

Music applied to objects of Passion, serves to embellish and aggrandise them, and make them enter, with a Pleasure unknown before, into the very Recesses of the Soul. It raises noble Hints, and opens the Mind to great Conceptions, furnishing it with a new capacity, as well as a new opportunity of satisfaction. But above all, it qualifies the Heart to receive the Influence of this important Consideration; we therein feel a lively sense of God's Goodness, and are taught to thank him for this, among other Instances of his kindness; this, one of the greatest Felicities of human Nature, a melodious Constitution.

Morell's work with Handel went from strength to strength. He wrote the text for *Theodora*, a non-Biblical subject which drew from Handel one of his greatest scores. When Morell asked him whether he did not look upon the 'Grand Chorus in the *Messiah*' as his masterpiece, he replied 'No, I think the chorus at the end of the second part in *Theodora* far beyond it', a judgment which many Handelians have been happy to endorse.

Handel's farewell to oratorio was *Jephtha* (1752), which Morell claimed to be his own particular favourite among the works on which he collaborated with the great man. Written during a time of failing sight and physical weariness, the oratorio is a reworking from the Old Testament of the legend of the man forced to kill his own child after vowing to sacrifice the first creature he sees should the gods grant him victory.

In chapter 11 of 'The Book of Judges', Jephtha's daughter dies, the sacrificial virgin child; in Morell's reworking, she is spared, bidden by an Angel from God to spend her days in nun-like seclusion. Handel evidently agreed to this piece of pious sentimentalism, though not for the first time in their collaboration, the music often defies the spirit of the text.

The breadth of Morell's reading is confirmed by the fact that his libretti are strewn with pickings and borrowings from the works of the great English poets. The very first chorus of *Jephtha* takes its character from the line 'In dismall dance around the furnace blue', lifted directly from Milton's *On the Morning of Christ's Nativity*. (Thomas Gray, a man 'by no means partial to Handel', particularly thrilled to this chorus.) At the heart of *Jephtha* stands the great chorus 'How dark, O Lord, are thy decrees!', a song of acceptance shot through with fatalism, anger, and despair. The grim final line 'Whatever is, is right' comes from Pope's *Essay on Man*. Morell had originally changed this to 'What God ordains is right' but Handel insisted on the original which he invests with an irony and indignation even Swift might have shuddered to contemplate.

*

Within a decade of Handel's death in 1759, his music was being neglected. *Sturm und Drang* was the new fashion; J. C. Bach was all the rage. It was this which in 1776 caused the Earl of Sandwich and a number of his friends from Eton days to found the 'The Noblemen's Concert of Antient Music' for the purpose of playing music that was at least twenty years old. The conductor was Joah Bates, another Old Etonian, who had been tutor to Sandwich's son at King's College, Cambridge.

The prospectus was written by Sir John Hawkins who complained that an addiction to the new merely made composers a slave to fashion. 'The Concert of Antient Music', he promised, would revel in a variety of styles and traditions: Byrd and Palestrina, Purcell and J. S. Bach, Avison and Corelli, Pergolesi and Handel. His prospectus also struck a moral note, '... the ingenuous youth, who prefers the innocent pleasures of music to riot and intemperance, may taste of that mirth which draws no repentance after it.' Goodness knows what the loose-living Earl of Sandwich made of this. When Thomas Gray heard that Sandwich was a candidate for the position of High Steward of Cambridge University in 1763, he wrote:

> They say he's no Christian, loves drinking and whoring,
> And all the town rings of his swearing and roaring

History has not looked kindly on John Montagu, 4th Earl of Sandwich (1718-92). Educated at Eton and Trinity College, Cambridge, after succeeding to the peerage at the age of 12, he is principally remembered for his years as First Lord of the Admiralty when financial maladministration and political jobbery (jobs for musicians being one of his more amiable indulgences) drained the navy of resources and ideas, leaving it sadly exposed when the American Colonies revolted. It was also a life touched with scandal. Sandwich's involvement in the prosecution of John Wilkes, his old friend from the Medmenham Hellfire Club, prompted Gray to dub him

Jemmy Twitcher (the grass in *The Beggar's Opera*). Of his many mistresses, the most celebrated, the actress Martha Ray, was shot dead by an infatuated clergyman, the Revd Mr Hackman, while leaving the opera at Covent Garden.

After women, music was the principal passion of Sandwich's life, making him one of the eighteenth century's most enthusiastic patrons. He himself danced and played the kettledrums, despite being famously uncoordinated. (It is said that when he offered to provide his Parisian dancing-master with an introduction to London society, the Frenchman replied, 'I should take it as a particular kindness if your Lordship would never tell anyone in London of whom you learned to dance'.) He also sang. In 1761 he founded the 'The Noblemen and Gentlemen's Catch Club' for the singing of canons, catches, and glees. The club, which survives today in what remains of the House of Lords, originally met on Tuesdays from February to June at the Thatched House Tavern. For the bicentenary in 1961, the composer Malcolm Arnold contributed a part-song.

Sandwich died in 1792. According to his obituarist in the *Gentleman's Magazine*, the cause of death was 'a diarrhoea which had been two years in operation'.

*

One of Lord Sandwich's shrewder pieces of musical patronage was the promotion of the career of Joah Bates (1740-99) who was variously his private secretary, tutor to his son, and the beneficiary of a number of sinecures. Sandwich's patronage enabled Bates to pursue a career as a keyboard player, conductor, and musical panjandrum, a career which reached its apogee in 1784 when he directed the mammoth Handel centenary festival in Westminster Abbey.

Bates was an example of that uncommon but by no means rare phenomenon, the north-countryman who arrives at Eton late and draws career-sustaining sustenance from what it has to offer. He was born in Halifax into a family which had ambitions to dominate the town's thriving musical community. He attended schools and studied with organists in Rochdale and Manchester before being elected at the age of sixteen to an Eton scholarship on 2 August, 1756.

In his entry on Bates in the *Dictionary of National Biography*, J. A. Fuller Maitland states that while Bates was at Eton 'he was deprived of music altogether, but he kept up his practice by playing on imaginary keys on the table'. This vastly misleading statement appears to be based on nothing more than the widely held assumption that no musical assistance was offered to boys at Eton pre-1860. Two contemporary sources tell otherwise.

Bates's obituary in the *Gentleman's Magazine* in June 1799 describes how he was taken under the wing of an assistant master, Mr George Graham, 'a man whose elegant scholarship and polite acquisitions introduced him to the friendship of the principal literary characters of his day'. Graham, we learn, became

. . . the voluntary tutor of Mr Bates, who, when the business of the Pupil-room was over, was encouraged to indulge his musical propensities at Mr Graham's harpsichord.

A biographical sketch published twelve years earlier in *The World* (its editor, Edward Topham, was at Eton in the 1760s) confirms the story, though in a way which is determined to show Graham in a less than flattering light:

JOAH BATES. – Was on the foundation, and has some merit as a scholar – but *industria magis quam ingenio* and he got forward, as he has done since by assiduity. For Graham, mad Graham was his tutor, and they were equally fond of music… They passed the greatest part of their time in musical application; and after a long search, on an exercise day, were found together in the organ loft at Chapel, lost in admiration of each other's talents.

Reports like this, with their veiled suggestions of oddity, obsession, and impropriety, would remain the stock-in-trade of masters and boys hostile to music and music-making in English public schools well into the twentieth century.

In the summer of 1758, Bates was elected to a scholarship at King's College, Cambridge. He took up residence in 1760 and was elected to a fellowship ten years later. He made his name initially as a keyboard player of rare accomplishment, a virtuoso whose playing was not confined to 'the notes, and nothing but the notes'. This, combined with his intelligence and relentless ambition, made him a force to be reckoned with.

He did, however, lose one major battle in his musical career. Returning to Halifax in 1767 to prepare a performance of *Messiah* with the local choir, he became embroiled in a ferocious controversy, the details of which have come down to us in a 28-page pamphlet entitled *A Plain and True Narrative of the Differences between Messrs B---S [Bates] and members of the Musical-Club, holden at the Old-Cock, in Halifax, in a letter to a friend.*

At the heart of the dispute was the Bates family's plan to take over the congenial, well-run Halifax music club and turn it into a high-powered, county-wide 'choral union' with its own resident organist whose appointment and funding the Bateses would control. (Many great nineteenth-century northern choirs would be established on just such a basis.)

Bates's visit was clearly intended to clinch the deal. In the event, it did the very reverse. Eton and Cambridge had given him airs, or so it seemed to the locals. When the choir asked for a break for refreshment during the first *Messiah* rehearsal, Bates responded with a supercilious sneer, 'I know they are dry Dogs but we must begin the second Act'. When relations further deteriorated, Bates 'began to lay aside Reason and Decency and descended down right to Scurrility and Abuse'. The locals, who smelled several rats when confronted with the Bates family take-over plan, dubbed Bates 'a designing, self-interested hypocrite'. He eventually left Halifax 'breathing a torrent of virulence, and scurrility', stamping the ground and crying 'I have laid the scoundrels low!', which was clearly not the case.

⋆

The Halifax debacle may have angered Bates but it was grist to his mill and stood him in good stead for dealing with the grandest undertaking of his career, the great Handel festival of 1784.[1]

The festival was planned 'over five or six dinners' in Bates's house in January 1783 by Bates himself, fellow Etonian Viscount Fitzwilliam, and Sir Watkin Williams Wynn. Patrons included Lord Sandwich and the music-loving George III. It was originally planned for Easter 1784 but a dissolution of parliament caused it to be delayed until 26-29 May, dates, it was subsequently agreed, that better suited 'persons of tender constitutions'. An evening concert of Handel's secular music

---

1 This was a year early. We now know that Handel was born in 1685 not 1684 as his memorial in Westminster Abbey misleadingly stated. 1784 was, however, the 25th anniversary of his death.

in James Wyatt's new 1600-seat Pantheon Theatre in Oxford Street (stifling, as it turned out, in the summer heat) was to be framed by daytime programmes of sacred music in Westminster Abbey.

The programme for the opening concert on Wednesday, 26 May reads:

I

The Dettingen *Te Deum*

II

Overture, with the Dead March in SAUL
Part of the FUNERARY ANTHEM
When the ear heard him
He delivered the poor that cried
His body is buried in peace
GLORIA PATRI, from JUBILATE

III

ANTHEM – O sing unto the Lord
CHORUS – The Lord shall reign
from ISRAEL IN EGYPT

Messiah performed by more than 500 singers and instrumentalists at noon on Saturday, 29 May provided the festival with its grandiose climax.

The programme book names 535 musicians – 275 singers and an orchestra of 260, led by Wilhelm Cramer [2] – under the central direction of Bates himself. James Wyatt, who was Surveyor of Westminster Abbey as well as architect of the Pantheon Theatre, was charged with seating this vast assembly of performers and an audience of between three and four

2 95 Violins I, 26 Violins II, 21 Cellos, 15 Double basses, 16 Flutes, 26 oboes, 27 bassoons, 12 horns, 12 trumpets, 6 trombones, 4 Kettledrums. 11 sopranos, 47 trebles, 48 [male] altos, 83 tenors, 84 basses, soloists.

thousand festival-goers. A royal box was constructed at the east end of the Abbey and a vast stepped tribune built at the west end for the instrumentalists, choirs, and organ. It is an earnest of the size of the tribune that the organ, by Green of Islington, was a new instrument destined for Canterbury Cathedral. After being assembled in Westminster Abbey, it was dismantled, boxed and reassembled in Canterbury.

Bates, seated at the base of a vast V-formation, directed from a harpsichord which was coupled to an organ by keys 'extending nineteen feet from the body of the organ, and twenty-seven inches below the perpendicular of the set of keys by which it usually played'. This was not a new device but it was the longest yet assembled.

Behind and below Bates were the soloists and choristers from Westminster Abbey itself, St Paul's Cathedral, the Chapel Royal, and St George's, Windsor. In the aisles to the left and right, rising up and disappearing from the public view, were more massed voices. Three subdirectors – ancillary time-beaters – were employed to assist Bates. In his *Musical Memoirs*, composer William Parke would recall the twelve tiers appearing

… to ascend to the clouds, united with the saints and martyrs represented in the stained glass of the west window… Perhaps no band of mortal musicians ever exhibited a more imposing appearance to the eye or afforded more ecstatic and affecting sounds to the ear than this.

Musicians came from all parts of the kingdom at their own expense to take part in the festival. Bates began the previous week with a 'sifting' of unaccredited singers (of 120 applicants only two were rejected) which he followed with a so-called 'drilling rehearsal' in the Tottenham Court Concert Room. There was one general rehearsal for each performance. Bates fumed and raged when five hundred people were admitted to the first of these general rehearsals but the income the audience yielded at half a sovereign a head, and the publicity it engendered, proved his assistants wiser than he. Within hours of the rehearsal's conclusion, the entire festival, rehearsals and all, was completely sold out.

Doors opened for the Abbey performances at 9 a.m. Such was the rage to secure the best seats, ladies of quality are said to have had their hair dressed the previous evening (how they slept is not vouchsafed). There were reports of 'dishevelled hair and torn garments' in the early-morning rush for seats but no serious harm was done. As Burney later reported, the quality of Wyatt's workmanship was demonstrated 'by the whole four days of commemoration in the Abbey being exempted from every species of accident'.

Musically, the Abbey performances were judged sensational by amateur and professional alike. Singer Michael Kelly would recall:

When I first heard the chorus of the 'Hallelujah' in the *Messiah*, and 'For unto us a child is born', my blood thrilled with rapturous delight; it was sublime, it was, in the inspired words of the chorus, 'Wonderful'.

Diarist Mary Hamilton wrote:

I was so delighted that I thought myself in the heavenly regions. 513 Performers, the Harmony so unbroken that it was like the fall of Waters from one source, imperceptibly blended. The Spectacle too was sublime, So universal a silence, So great a number of People.

Burney himself commented on the silences: 'no single cannon was ever fired with more exact precision' and again 'the silence was so awful and entire, as if none but the tombs of departed mortals had been present'.

In his heart of hearts, Burney disapproved deeply of the whole venture. He believed that in choosing to perform *Messiah* with 500 or more musicians, Bates, Sandwich and their co-conspirators against musical sense had muddled up the smaller forces, which Handel himself naturally looked to, with those that had been used on grand state occasions such as the coronation of George II. In this, he credited George III with slightly more sense than the organisers:

His Majesty's partiality for Handel's music was generally spoken of; but I believe it was not universally known what an excellent and accurate judge he was of its merits. The fine chorus of 'Lift up your heads, O ye gates', was always given in full chorus, and indeed intended to be so given by Handel. The king suggested that the first part of it should be made a semi-chorus and sung only by the principal singers; but when it came to the passage, 'He is the King of Glory!' he commanded that the whole orchestra, with the full chorus, should, with a tremendous forte burst out; the effect produced by the alteration was awful and sublime.

Years later Burney was still harbouring dark thoughts as to how 'the double drums, double curtals, tromboni &c. augmented his lordship's [Lord Sandwich's] pleasure in proportion to the din and stentorophonic screams of these truly savage instruments'. In practice, he thrilled to the event and eventually wrote the definitive account of it [3] in which he paid tribute to the astonishing quality of ensemble achieved by Bates:

So it seems as if the magnitude of the band had commanded and impelled adhesion and obedience beyond that of any inferior force. The pulsations in every limb, and ramifications of veins and arteries in an animal, could not be more reciprocal, isochronous, and under the

3 *An Account of the Musical Performances in Westminster Abbey and the Pantheon in Commemoration of Handel* (London, 1785).

regulation of the heart, than the members of this body of Musicians and that conductor [Bates] and leader [Cramer].

So proud was Burney of what eventually turned out to be both a record of the festival and a learned monograph on Handel that he read parts of it to the hated Sandwich. This was a mistake. Though Burney had received royal permission to publish, Sandwich stipulated that all the profits from Burney's book should go, along with the profits of the event itself, to the Fund for Decayed Musicians. Burney agreed with an ill-grace. As he later recalled, 'I fretted afterwards, & grumbled in the gizzard'.

The three rehearsals and performances, and the two additional performances of *Messiah* on 3 and 5 June, grossed £12,736. 12s. 10d. Wyatt's bill came to £1,969. 12s. 0d., band expenses were £1,971. 17s. 0d., programmes cost £262. 15s. 0d. After sundry expenses and a donation from George III of £525, £7,000 was raised for good causes. £6,000 went to the Society of Decayed Musicians, £1,000 to Westminster Hospital.

Bates himself was not so fortunate financially. In 1791, he and his Halifax-born wife Sarah Bates, a distinguished oratorio singer, lost virtually all their savings when a fire gutted the Albion Mills. The night after the fire, he is said to have 'assisted at a concert with his usual spirit and attention' but it must have been a serious blow.

Bates was one of the most remarkable performing musicians of the eighteenth century. Moreover, he has a strong claim, on the basis of the 1784 Handel festival, to being one of the first identifiable orchestral and choral 'conductors' in the modern sense of the word. Sadly (former denizens of the Old-Cock in Halifax might say 'happily'), Eton has yet to produce a second Joah Bates.

An operatic birching

In earlier times, Eton enjoyed a robust reputation for the severity of its floggings, a reputation which reached its apogee during the headmastership of Keate, 'that genial flagellant' as someone once called him. It is not surprising, therefore, to find in the British Library a slim quarto volume entitled *The Opera Il penseroso (i.e the operation of birching). A performance both vocal and instrumental, as it is acted at the Royal theatres of Eton and Westminster, etc.* The Argument announces:

The Performance has had a longer Run than any Thing ever yet exhibited on the Stage, as it has always *acted* for the *Benefit* (though not the *Entertainment*) of several juvenile Societies.

DRAMATIS PERSONAE

PAIDAGOGOS, the *Principal Actor*,
GRAPPLE,
ROD,
BLOCK,
   And,
BLOCKHEAD

Act the First or Second, or Third, or as often as there shall be Occasion.
SCENE wherever you please to make it.
Guards, Attendants, &c.   *Exeunt.*

After the proper *Overture*, Curtain draws and discovers,

There follows a coloured engraving of a beating and four lines of doggerel, crudely notated and clearly not intended for performance.

> Birch and green Holly
> Birch and green Holly
> If thou be'st beaten, Boy
> Thank thine own Folly

The meat in this somewhat spare satirical repast is to be found in the Argument itself, which is full of puns and *double entendres*.

The ancients were wont to represent each character in a mask; but here our hero must be *unmasked*, that no *tender part* may *unfeelingly* be passed over... With respect to the musical performance... as it is usual to *score the fundamental parts*, the musical connoisseur may be gratified in this particular, if he chuses it: though indeed the *vocal part* is difficult to be expressed, as it consists of *tremulous* and *chromatic strains*, and other *movements*, abounding in *rapid Italick flights* from the *bottom* to the top, the spirit of which greatly depends on the *instrumental accompaniment*.

The date of this sado-musical *jeu d'esprit* is uncertain. The library catalogue suggests *c*.1790.

CHAPTER 5

Masquerades

Long Chamber, which for four centuries was the lodging-place-cum-dormitory of the King's Scholars, was as famous for its theatricals and masquerades as it was notorious for other aspects of its regime. The masquerades seem to have been especially lively in the early years of the nineteenth century with, once again, clear evidence of a greater degree of musical sophistication among Etonians of the period than has generally been assumed.

The Revd C. A. Wilkinson, a former captain of College, is the principal source of information from this period. He writes of one masquerade:

There was a Scotch lassie with 'herrings, caller herring', there was a jolly Italian boy dancing the *Tarantella* to his 'hurdy-gurdy'; there was a Scotch beggar with his bagpipes and that most excruciating of all music to any but a native's ear; there was a Jew old-clothes man, with four old top hats one on top of the other; in fact, there were representatives of the traders from the 'Seven Dials' and other back slums, with most of the 'cries of Old London', and a stunning discord of all kinds of – so-called – music. But some of course soared higher. There was a trim finnikin sixth-form in green velvet or velveteen tunic, the orthodox plumed hunter's hat, brown tights and yellow boots, with long false hair and moustaches, doing Caspar in [Weber's] *Der Freischütz*.

The operatic reference is by no means surprising. We know from the journal of Charles Metcalfe, later Lord Metcalfe, who entered Eton in 1796 aged eleven, of the astonishing sophistication of some Etonians of the period.[1]

What was perhaps the most talked-about masquerade in Wilkinson's time took place towards the end of 1832. It was based on the character of Dr Dulcamara, the mountebank in Eugène Scribe's *opéra-comique*, *Le philtre*, which was first performed, to music by Auber, at the Paris Opéra in June 1831 and which Donizetti turned into his droll and affecting opera *L'elisir d'amore* the following year. In the opera, Dulcamara makes his appearance on stage in a cart drawn by a donkey. For the masquerade, Wilkinson hired both a costume and a donkey, the latter through the 'chief cad', a bibulous former cricketer and professional bruiser by the name of Picky Powell.

Since the Head Master patrolled College at 7.30 p.m. and again at 8, Wilkinson arranged to take delivery of the donkey from the end of what is now Keate's Lane at 7.45. Lured forward by a bunch of carrots, the donkey was led through School Yard and up the staircase into Lower Chamber where it was concealed in the captain's study until the Head Master had completed his rounds. Finally, it was heaved and pushed up the stairs into Long Chamber where gimcrack wares were dispensed from its saddlebags and a picnic was served during which 'the donkey came in for a share of viands that had never fallen to a donkey's lot before'.

No music featured in the escapade but the fact that Wilkinson had even heard of the piece – the Parisian *Le philtre* or the Milanese *L'elisir d'amore* – suggests sophisticated contacts and an unusually informed interest in musical theatre.

1 Metcalfe read Ariosto, Gibbon, and Voltaire, enquired into the authenticity of Chatterton's poems, translated Rousseau, drew, wrote poetry, and is said to have introduced to Eton the custom of inviting like-minded friends to afternoon tea.

CHAPTER 6

A moiety of Mudge

It is difficult to derive much pleasure from what one reads of worship and music in Eton College Chapel in the first half of the nineteenth century. Real change would not come until the 1860s when pressure was exercised by two formidable external sources: the Clarendon Commission on Public Schools and the 85-year-old Miss Maria Hackett.

In Maria Hackett's case, it had not been for want of trying earlier. A tireless campaigner for church music, for choir schools in particular,[1] she was 30 when, in 1813, she got wind of an official enquiry into the abuse of College statutes by Eton Fellows. The enquiry, which was primarily concerned with the holding of livings outside Eton, absolved the Fellows of serious wrong-doing but Miss Hackett remained unconvinced. In her view, Eton's blatant disregard of the statutes concerning the chapel choir was a far more serious matter where the day-to-day well-being of the school was concerned.

In 1818, she circulated a letter to a number of people, including the Provost, Joseph Goodall. Goodall was wary of circulars but, convinced of Miss Hackett's good faith, agreed

1 *The Times* (obituary, 5 November, 1874) described Miss Hackett as an accomplished classical scholar, an ardent lover of cathedral music, and the kindest friend to young choristers, frequently paying for private music lessons where she found talent. 'In the autumn of each year, she made a six-week tour of the cathedral towns, always carrying presents for the choirboys, whose names she knew and kept in a diary, usually giving each boy a book and a shilling. Her interest and judicious exertions created great reforms in schools and also in the treatment of choirboys.'

to respond to her 'off the record'. He conceded that *prima facie* the College was in breach of its statutes but argued that common sense suggested, and good faith would concede, that circumstances had changed out of all recognition since the fifteenth century. The choir, he acknowledged, was now based in Windsor but shared between St George's Chapel and Eton. The ten choristers – admitted at the age of six and retained until their voices broke – were taught music, reading, and arithmetic, with Eton contributing to the funding of a schoolmaster and an organist. Allowances of meat, bread and beer were also made by Eton and a grant of £5 paid towards each boy's being found an apprenticeship when he left the choir. (Goodall thought this insufficient and later trebled it to £15.)

Needless to say, none of this addressed the central question of Eton being in default of its statutes by no longer having choristers on its roll eligible for election to the foundation. Miss Hackett persisted, Provost Goodall tired of her persistence; and there, for the time being, the matter rested.

*

By the early 1800s, Eton was making relatively little use of the Windsor choir. Daily services in Eton Chapel had long been abandoned. Eton boys attended twice on Sundays and whole holidays, and in the afternoon on half-holidays. (The latter little more than an ill-disguised roll-call.) The St George's choir sang Sunday Evensong and so-called 'surplice services' on whole holidays.

The quality of the St George's Choir improved noticeably after the appointment of the 20-year-old George (later Sir

George) Elvey to Windsor in 1835. Famous among the men Elvey appointed was the tenor Charles Lockey, one of Mendelssohn's favourite singers; infamous was the bass, Mr Bridgewater, better known as 'Thunderguts'. Bridgewater's coarse and aggressive singing was a huge aggravation to several generations of Etonians, among them the future Poet Laureate, Robert Bridges, who greeted news of his death with an amusing but unforgiving verse obituary.

Epitaph on a Gentleman of the Chapel Royal

Old Thunderg---s is dead, we weep for that,
He sings for aye his lowest note, B flat.
Unpursed his mouth, empty his mighty chest,
His run is o'er, and none may bar his rest.
We hope he is not d-----d, for if he be,
He's on the wrong side of the middle sea.
Nay, we are sure, if weighed, he will not fail
Against the devil to run down the scale
While e'en three-throated Cerberus must retreat
From that which bellows from his sixteen feet;
Or should he meet with Peter at the door,
He'll seize the proper key as heretofore,
And by an easy turn he'll quickly come
From common time straight to *ad libitum*.
There in the equal temperament of Heaven,
Sharps, crotchets, accidentals, all forgiven,
He'll find his place directly, and perspire
Among the basses of the Elysian quire.
Fear, dwellers on the earth, this acquisition
To the divine ethereal ammunition;
A thunder is let loose, a very wonder
Of earthborn, pitiless, Titanic thunder;
We, who remain below and hear his roar,
Must kneel and tremble where we laughed before.

A particular bone of contention where the Windsor choir was concerned was the choir's habit of processing early out of Sunday Evensong at Eton in order to prepare for Evensong at St George's. This was at a time when the egregiously named Mr Mudge was one of the Windsor Lay Clerks. At a Founder's Day dinner, one of the Eton Fellows, Harry Dupuis, is said to have complained, 'Mr Provost, this state of things is intolerable. I, for one, protest against our having only a moiety of Mudge.'

The Eton Fellows added their own share of misery to Eton services. Their sermons were famously poor, their demeanour generally unimpressive. One Fellow was pilloried in verse:

> Didactic, dry, declamatory, dull;
> Big bellied, bellows like a bull.

As for Eton's chapel functionaries, they, too, seem to have made a sorry impression. The organist, John Mitchell, was said to be a charitable man 'for his right hand knoweth not what his left hand doeth'. The Parish Clerk, John Gray, had an unpleasant voice and an even more unpleasant habit of expectorating on his hands prior to tolling the chapel bell.

*

The sorry state of Eton's chapel life c.1840 contrasted with the school's successes elsewhere. It also revealed the degree to which a gulf had opened between Christianity and Classicism in Eton's psyche. In pre-Renaissance Catholic Eton, Latin and Greek served a largely practical function. In post-Renaissance, Anglican, free-wheeling, free-spirited Eton the teaching of the classics offered classical humanism as an alternative to religious ideology.

No one who is familiar with the life of the poet Shelley can be in any doubt as to the degree to which the English classical education of the time – what Cyril Connolly would later call 'the Eleusinian mysteries of learning'– empowered the abler students: honing their minds and exposing them at an early age to the best that had been thought and created in poetry, drama, philosophy, politics and science. The young Shelley is usually portrayed as a dangerous rebel during his time at Eton, a disaffected pagan. There is some truth in this. What the portrait omits to include is the extraordinary benefits the Eton education conferred on him.

*

During the 1840s the ancient English Public Schools were challenged by a sudden proliferation of new foundations. Arnold's reforms at Rugby and the Oxford Movement within the Anglican Church were the twin forces driving this new educational revolution. Schools founded in the 1840s, or shortly afterwards, included: Cheltenham (1841), Marlborough (1843), Rossall (1844), Radley (1847), Lancing (1848), Hurstpierpoint (1849), Bradfield (1850), St John's Leatherhead (1851), Wellington (1853).

In a limited way, these Victorian foundations were following the same path Eton had trod four centuries earlier. The chapel was central to the idea of each school and at Lancing, Radley, and Bradfield music was integral to the idea of the chapel. The Revd Nathaniel Woodard, who founded Lancing, was famously obsessed with the improving power of Gregorian chant. The Revd Thomas Stevens, Rector of Bradfield, began his own particular educational odyssey by inviting a former Reading church organist, John Binfield, to teach 'the whole village to sing by note'. After commissioning architect Gilbert Scott to redesign and extend the village church, Stevens founded St Andrew's College, Bradfield to provide its choir.

For all their manifest failings, Eton's Provost and Fellows were not unmindful of the changes which were taking place elsewhere. It cannot be entirely coincidental that two massive projects were put in train at the end of the 1840s: the rehousing of the King's Scholars and a large-scale renovation of College Chapel which involved the temporary erection of a wooden church, complete with stained glass, on Fellows' Eyot. Alas, the renovated chapel with its new Gray and Davison organ – a visual mess with its fake tin pipes but 'prompt, clear, and forcible in speech' – did not noticeably improve what went on within the building.

'We were a cold, stagnant, mute congregation,' conceded Arthur Coleridge, the barrister and amateur musician who later went on to found the Bach Choir. 'And the boys' behaviour was far from uplifting'. There was much talking and eating in chapel. Almonds and raisins were routinely passed round by the aristocratic *élite* who were now provided with their own stalls. It was not unusual to see a boy saunter-ing into divine service with his cricket bat under his arm. At confirmation, the confirmands and their families were seated below the choir. On one such occasion, the tenor John Hobbs was some way into the sublime recitative which prefaces Handel's 'Comfort ye, my people' when he let out a yowl of pain. Since he was a stoutish, thick-set party, it was assumed he had suffered some kind of seizure. In fact, a small dog belong-ing to one of the confirmands, a young colleger, had sunk its teeth into the great man's thigh.

Hymns were routinely abused by the boys. A favourite device was substituting the names of watermen and loafers on the Thames:

> Jack Haverley,
> Bob Tolliday,
> Row all the day
> Round Surley Bay!
> Amen.

There were boys who would have wished it otherwise but who quickly learned to keep their counsel. A friend of Arthur Coleridge by the name of Randall was unwise enough to whisper at the start of the *Magnificat*: 'Arthur, my grandfather's service in B flat'. Thereafter any music which did not please the assembled bloods was met with the line: 'Randall will be licked for his grandfather's bad anthem'.

Henry Salt later rationalised the situation by blaming misconduct in chapel on 'the long and wearisome choral services, beautiful in themselves, but quite unsuited to the majority of boys'. There is no evidence that they were 'beautiful in themselves'. ('Noble music badly sung and worse played' was the judgment of the musically aware Oscar Browning who was in College from 1851-6.) The musically inclined took their pleasures elsewhere. It was not unusual in Victorian times for Eton boys to eavesdrop on Evensong at St George's Chapel before racing down the hundred steps beneath the castle battlements and back across the river to answer their names at 'absence'.

Song for the Fourth of June

William Johnson Cory, one of the most celebrated of all Eton masters and the author of the words of the *Eton Boating Song*, had a distinctive taste in music. Military band music was a particular passion. 'Brats! The British Army!' he would cry whenever this particular musical intoxicant came within earshot of his schoolroom on the High Street. Like many a King's Scholar, both before and since, Johnson had no use for the usual. In 1878, six years after his mysteriously abrupt departure from Eton, he wrote to Arthur Coleridge who had recently founded the Bach Choir:

How persevering you are, how inconvertible. I regard the study of Bach as most laudable like the transit of Venus or the bottled *infusoria*, or the challenged dredge; but I am personally content to cry at *Madame Angot* [Lecocq], and even the *Grande Duchesse* [Offenbach], still more at *Lochabar* played by the Scots Guards. What is Bach to me? Just what he would have been to Burns. *Vide* Burns.

When, at Oscar Wilde's prompting, F. R. Benson staged Aeschylus's *Agamemnon* at Oxford in 1880, Johnson wrote:

It is a very odd event; it would bore me worse than Handel's *Messiah* . . The only really interesting Greek tragedy, the only one in which one cares a twopenny damn what is going to happen, is *Philoctetes*.

In his later years, Johnson changed his name to Cory, moved to Madeira, married, sired a son and settled in Hampstead where he died, aged 69, in June 1892. Looking back over the best part of sixty years, he picked out the musical experiences he had found most affecting:

Last scene of *Ernani*, Patti in *Il barbiere di Siviglia*, Christine's first utterance in *Faust*, girls' chorus in *Mireille*, a fiddler striking at the Ticino Ferry (Lake Lugano) just as I looked up the long water-line and saw the snow at the end of it, in 1832 the *Duc de Reichstadt's Waltz* [Johann Strauss the Elder] on Windsor Terrace, in 1876 *Lochabar* Scots Guards at St James's.

Johnson wrote the words of the Boating Song while ill in Torquay during the Christmas vacation of 1862-3. On 9 January, 1863 he wrote to his brother:

I could not get to sleep last night, being engaged in making a half-humorous, half-sentimental boating song for the 4th of June; and when I wake I find it burning to be written out. I do a song with a tune in my head, perhaps two; last night it was 'Waiting for the Wagon' and 'A Health to the Outward Bound'.

The text first appeared in *The Eton Scrap-Book* III on 5 June, 1865. Six days later Johnson wrote to one of his former pupils, Algernon Drummond, who was currently stationed with the Rifle Brigade in Lahore:

Everard [the younger brother of Lord Dalmeny, afterwards 5th Earl of Rosebery] is joint editor of a new periodical called 'Eton Scrapbook': the third, probably last [not so] number on the 6th June, and was much better than the second: he insisted on printing therein the song which you had copied, about the revel [Boats' supper], but no one has taken the least notice of the elaborate rhymes [in 3, 4, 5 stanzas: all omitted in the song], which cost the writer untold pangs in the winter of 1862-3.

Drummond had been in Evans's from 1857-61. He was not a musician himself but he had a passion for music not dissimilar to Johnson's. One of his happiest memories of Eton was perching in his window-seat above Keate's Lane listening to a barrel organ playing tunes from Verdi's *Il trovatore* in the street below. Operatic arias and 'the higher kinds of ballad' could also be heard in the drawing-room at Evans's where the Vidal family held court.[1]

Drummond's mind was so well stocked with memorable melodies, it is perhaps not surprising that he should have come up with a tune apt to Johnson's hauntingly evocative *barcarolle*. A fellow officer in the Rifle Brigade, Thomas Mitchell-Innes, helped write the melody down and the celebrated Boating Song was born. In a letter written more than fifty years later, Drummond modestly recalled:

I was haunted by the words and the tune (I think partly founded on a setting of Blockley's for Tennyson's 'Break, break' which I heard at the time) came into my head. We had several Old Etonians in the battalion and sang it often at Mess after dinner. A brother officer took down the notes. After I came home in 1869 a cousin of mine, Miss Evelyn Wodehouse... wrote an accompaniment for it, and it was published by Ollivier in Bond Street [in 1878]. Later on, as Ollivier had retired from business, John Roberts asked leave to publish it as a waltz [the Drummond/Mitchell-Innes original is in 6/8 time, 'In tempo di Barcarola'], and eventually bought the copyright [for £10]. The royalties are now paid to the Bursar and supply the Drummond-Cory music-prize.

Though Etonians nowadays occasionally affect indifference towards the song, there is no denying the fact that Johnson's amusing and affecting poem is complemented by one of the great national melodies. As with *Greensleeves* or the famous tune in the Trio of Elgar's *Pomp and Circumstance*

1 Lily Vidal married Edward Stone. Their son, Christopher Stone, presented music programmes for the BBC in the pioneering days of broadcasting. Their daughter, Faith, married the novelist Compton Mackenzie, founder of *The Gramophone*.

March No. 1, confidence, calm and a sense of understated aspiration are met with a mood of quiet melancholy which, before the onset of the aural mayhem of our present age, it was possible to recognise as being peculiarly and quintessentially English.

CHAPTER 7

Hubert Parry

In 1861, the year the Palmerston government began its deliber-
ations on the constitutions and conduct of the ancient Public
Schools, there arrived in Eton a boy who would effect a musical revolution of his own within the school. His name was
Hubert Parry. Over the next five years, he astonished his
contemporaries with his musical achievements and – more
remarkably, since he had an erratic heart condition – his
sporting ones.

Parry came from a well-to-do Gloucestershire family but
the circumstances were hardly propitious. His father, Thomas
Gambier Parry, was a widower,[1] his brother, the 21-year-old
Charles Clinton Parry, was an emotionally disturbed wastrel.[2]
In November 1861, only months after Parry had arrived at
Eton, his 19-year-old sister, Lucy, died of consumption as her
mother had done before her. Misfortune even afflicted
Hubert's immediate circle of friends at school. That same
year, the father of George Herbert – the 13th Earl of Pembroke, whose sister, Maude, Parry would eventually marry –
also died, exhausted by his humanitarian work in the Crimea.

Parry was palpably dismayed by the state of Eton music in

1 Anna Parry (1816-48) had died of consumption shortly after giving birth to
Hubert.
2 Charles Clinton Parry (1840-83) preceded Hubert to Eton. He was musically
gifted but suffered from mental illness: schizophrenia in all probability. At Oxford,
he became involved in drink, drugs and militant atheism, and was sent down.

1861. Mitchell's incompetence as organist seemed to know no bounds and chapel services often degenerated into chaos. A Parry diary entry reports:

First in the Psalms old Mitchell began wandering about on the keys, as if he had lost his place, and played the chant wrong all the way through. Then when the *Magnificat* began it seemed as if he was gone quite mad ... The choir began to sing snatches of the *Magnificat* at intervals, trying to make out what he was doing; this went on in the most hopeful manner for full three minutes, till one of the choirmen (Adams) went and stopped him, and made him play a chant. The whole chapel was convulsed, it was useless to try and prevent it.

We should not conclude from this, however, that the school as a whole was adrift. Parry's most recent biographer is wrong on several counts when he writes of 'the level of academic apathy and philistinism which existed in Eton in the 1860s, and was to undergo little change for the rest of the century'.[3] Academically, the school was in remarkably good shape.[4] In an ideal world, Parry might have had a less mordant, less disinterested tutor than Russell Day, though no one doubted Day's scholarly credentials. The tradition of the best Etonians being thoroughly well read also persisted; Parry's interest in madrigals and part-songs was rooted in the huge amount of poetry he read at Eton, from Edmund Spenser onwards.

The first glimmerings of a musical renaissance at Eton came with the founding of a Musical Society – a singing club,

3 Jeremy Dibble, *C.Hubert H. Parry: His Life and Music* (Oxford, 1992), p. 20.
4 See *Eton College Chronicle* 5 May, 1864, where the academic results of Etonians at Oxford and Cambridge, as published by the Public Schools Commission itself, are discussed. In one table, Eton is first out of the nine schools under review; in the other table, it is third. The only truly dismal results are Westminster's. After reading a newspaper article on the commission's work, Parry wrote in his diary, 'Westminster seems an awful place'.

in effect – in 1861. It failed for lack of funds but was refounded the following year by Parry, Eddie Hamilton, Spencer Lyttelton and others. The appointment to Eton of John Foster, a lay clerk at Westminster Abbey, as singing master greatly helped, though the state of the Society, along with the appalling quality of hymn-singing in Chapel, was a frequent topic of concern in the *Eton College Chronicle* in Parry's time.

Parry went to Elvey in Windsor to study music. Elvey lacked distinction as a composer but he was a fine tutor to the young man. He did, however, tend to reinforce Parry's own as yet somewhat conservative views on contemporary music. Early diary entries from Parry's Eton days often have a disapproving, priggish air. After a visit to the Three Choirs Festival in Hereford in August 1864, he reflected:

Rossini's *Stabat mater* I was thoroughly disgusted with. It is no more fit to be played in a sacred building than a quadrille. The 'quando corpus' and last chorus are fine. The last chorus particularly so. But it is not a good fugue.

As late as 1866, he is able to accuse Meyerbeer's *Les Huguenots*, which he had seen at Covent Garden, of containing 'a frightful amount of row and a great deal of bosh'. Mendelssohn was Parry's god, as he was Elvey's. A diary entry from 1865 describes Mendelssohn's 'Why rage fiercely' as being 'almost too glorious'. That, and a deeply impressive sermon by Samuel Wilberforce, provided Parry with an unlooked for double delight in College Chapel.

It was inevitable perhaps that Parry would eventually show flashes of impatience with Elvey's teaching. A setting of *Nunc dimittis* received its own dismission from Elvey – 'rather wild' – a judgment which did not please the young man. The fact is,

Parry's musical horizons were beginning to open wide. His response to Beethoven's music is guarded at first (the Eighth Symphony is described in his diary as 'intellectually challenging') but soon his own robust and rumbustious taste is showing through. Hearing the Fifth Symphony for the first time he writes 'words cannot express the hopeless gloriousness of this old ruffian... so tremendously massive'.

The many recitals and concerts Parry and his friends gave during his time at Eton were generally well supported by the establishment. Provost Goodford was a regular attender and a handful of masters could be relied upon to be there, Oscar Browning the leader of the pack. Programmes, too, became more adventurous. A chamber orchestra was founded which attempted some far-from-easy repertory: the overtures to Weber's *Der Freischütz* and Rossini's *Semiramide*, the second and fourth movements of Beethoven's First Symphony, and the last three movements of his Second Symphony. What is more, it was a contagion which was spreading. In 1866, the year Parry left Eton, there was even a Lower School concert.

At the same time, Parry was performing endless feats of derring-do in those two odd and occasionally violent pastimes unique to Eton, the Wall Game and the Field Game. He played the Wall Game with distinction and would have been Keeper of the Oppidan Wall had he not already been Keeper of the Field. He was frequently injured in these encounters. The injuries ranged from cut shins and sprained ankles to severe concussion. After one game, he was carried off unconscious on a sheep-hurdle. Straw was laid in Keate's Lane to dampen the noise of the traffic as he lay ill in the sickroom.

Though Parry was normally well ahead of himself academically, his numerous injuries often caused him to miss school. In Eton it is called 'staying out' and it is doubtful whether any Etonian has made better use of 'staying out' than Parry. We find him devouring Dickens (*The Pickwick Papers* and *Martin Chuzzlewit*, 'the most perfectly delightful book I ever read'), marvelling afresh at Shakespeare (*Twelfth Night*), revising an old part-song 'Tell us where is fancy bred?' or playing the organ to Robert Bridges. In the autumn of 1865, after being knocked unconscious in a football match, he spent his time in the sanatorium writing his *Overture in B minor* (a somewhat Mendelssohnian piece after the manner of the *Hebrides* Overture) which he and Eddie Hamilton played in a two-piano arrangement at a Musical Society concert the following December.

The diary entries reveal a bewildering array of physical activities. On 5 February, 1866 he plays 'a most utterly humbugging game of fives'; a fortnight later he is running the Steeplechase. Since the ground is flooded, he runs along the railway viaduct, shinning down a telegraph pole to get off. He strains his back throwing the hammer but is soon down in Windsor marvelling at Handel's 'When the ear heard him' at a funeral in St George's Chapel.

In the summer of 1866, he joined his first water party, hiring a boat at Maidenhead and rowing up to Cliveden:

When we got there, some of us rowed to the locks to bathe... and came down in time for a grand luncheon or dinner given in the little house that has been built on purpose for water parties for the Duchess of Sutherland. All the food came from Gunter's and was awfully good...We started afterwards to come down... We sang catches and part songs at different intervals all the way down. I had to sing alto and row all the way as well. When we got down near Windsor, about 9.30 – a beautiful starlit night – we sang lots of Mendelssohn's Part Songs 'open air music' which was very delightful. We got all safe to Windsor and left the party on Windsor Hill. Proceeded to the tobacconist, and ended up the day with cigars and beer on the Brocas, and went in very tired at about 10.30 – a most glorious day.

This contrasts pleasantly with an extraordinary piece of rowdyism in which Parry was involved that same summer after playing cricket for the 2nd XI against Winchester:

We had glorious fun coming back… We had a frightful row… smashed the window of the carriage, and we tore our blinds to pieces, and threw lemonade bottles out of the window… When we got to Windsor I fell in with Buckland and Scarlett, and we went down town together. At the door of the station, I picked up a bell, and ran up the hill ringing it hard. Campbell then took it up and threw it in the air; and then we kicked it down the hill: from whence it was taken and deposited in Barnes Pool. Buckland and I bowled over two drunkards at the door of the 'Swan', had a row with a soldier, tried the knockers and pulled all the bells. I bagged a large notice board and brought it all the way down town and deposited in Barnes Pool. After this we shouted ourselves hoarse and then went to our several houses and to bed. The next morning (June 30) the Station Master and porter appeared to complain; so we gave the porter the clapper, and told him he had better look for the bell at the bottom of Barnes Pool. Duff-Gordon, who threw the bell into Barnes Pool, was in an awful fright. He said we were all going to be expelled, particularly the boy who bagged the bell. However, that didn't come off, as I am still here (July 18).

Having escaped expulsion, Parry ended his time at Eton laden with honours. The *Eton College Chronicle* duly recorded the fact that he had been awarded his Oxford B.Mus. while still at Eton and that two of his works were now in print: 'Prevent us, O Lord' (4s.) and 'Blessed is he whose unrighteousness is forgiven' (1s.6d.). At his final Musical Society concert he sang the 'Pro peccatis' from Rossini's *Stabat mater*, the work he had earlier excoriated, and was obliged to repeat it as an encore. He received no fewer than 160 leaving-books, the most treasured of which was a handsomely bound copy of Tennyson's *Maud* from his friend 'Goosie', known to the wider world as Martin Le Marchant Gosselin. Parry left Eton on 14 December, 1866 alongside his friend of five years' standing, George Herbert, now Earl of Pembroke. He wrote in his diary:

Came away with George at 3. I watched the old place from the train until I couldn't see it any more; and so now I have done with the happiness of school life. I don't at all comprehend it, and I think it's a good thing I don't.

It is probably true to say that there have been few more extraordinary Etonian careers, as Eton itself recognised. At his funeral in St Paul's Cathedral on 16 October, 1918 Parry's coffin was borne by nine Etonians led, symbolically, by the Keeper of the Field.

*

Parry was no professional old boy but he did continue to serve the school. In 1891 he set Swinburne's Ode *Eton* written for the College's 450th anniversary. It is a nostalgic, occasionally triumphalist piece with a moving central interlude 'Still the reaches of the river, still the light on field and hill'. In 1908 he set Robert Bridges's *Eton Memorial Ode*, for the opening by King Edward VII of School Hall, dedicated to the memory of the 129 Etonians who died in the Boer War. The music, which quotes 'Assembly' and 'Fall in', is most affecting in those lines where Bridges addresses war's human cost:

Remember the love of them who came not home from the war,
The fatherly tears and the veiled faces.

Parry's diary entry for the day strikes a somewhat breezier note: 'Ode vigorously sung. Boys delightful – I loved them...'

In a lecture in Birmingham 1905, Edward Elgar made some famously slighting remarks about his English contemporaries. Parry, though, was exempted from criticism: 'with him no cloud of formality can dim the healthy and broad influence he exerts and we hope may long continue to exert upon us'. It was a very different judgment from that which had been made by George Bernard Shaw in *The World* in 1894:

Dr Parry occupies a position in the history of English art not unlike that occupied by Charles I in English politics. Any objection to his public compositions is immediately met by a reference to the extraordinary amiability of his private character. It is my firm belief that Hampden himself would have paid any assessment of Ship Money rather than sit out *Judith* a second time; and the attempt to arrest the five members seems a trifle in comparison with *Job*. But the defence is always the same – that Dr Parry sums up in person every excellence that the best type of private gentleman can pretend to do.

Parry was no Elgar or Vaughan Williams but he was a first-rate composer of the second rank[5] who had a powerful influence on both men, on Vaughan Williams in particular. It was Parry who had enjoined Vaughan Williams 'to write choral music as befits an Englishman and a democrat', as Parry himself would famously do when he set Blake's 'Jerusalem'.[6] Parry believed that music should never be merely illustrative; it should have

5 One of Parry's most characteristic works is his *Symphonic Variations* (see pp. 119-20). It is an earnest of his taste and generosity that, two years after the work's première in 1897, he was urging the performance and publication of Elgar's 'rival' *Enigma Variations*, a work which he held in the highest regard from the outset.
6 See p. 136-7.

'bottom', solidity of purpose. In his obituary of Parry in 1918, Vaughan Williams wrote:

Is a nation given over to frivolity and insincere vulgarity? We shall surely see it reflected in the music of that nation. There was no distinction for him between a moral and an artistic problem.

CHAPTER 8

Oscar Browning's nemesis

Parry's arrival at Eton coincided with the appointment to the teaching staff of Oscar Browning, a former King's Scholar who had been at Eton between 1851-6 when music was truly in the doldrums. Music affected Browning deeply. At the age of 16, he wrote:

Good music quite carries me away, it completely fills me. I forget that I am a man or walk on the earth. The really most affecting music I have heard was at Antwerp at the Church of the Augustins. It was a fête day. The moment the procession entered the church the organ began, and with the organ the whole orchestra. I was never so entranced.

Browning was a zealous amateur pianist whose playing was more ponderous than nimble. His legs were so short, they barely reached the pedals. As a result, the sustaining pedal, once identified, tended to be depressed for some time. He played duets with Parry ('I wish you and Parry wouldn't thump so' complained a visiting mother) and was never so happy as when playing the treble-part in an arrangement of a Beethoven symphony, swaying from the waist upwards like a man possessed and frequently turning to his partner to enquire whether he shared Browning's opinion that the whole experience was awfully jolly. He taught himself theory, founded his own choir at Eton which failed for lack of decent trebles, and organised numerous musical evenings which he planned with meticulous care, fussing over the programmes to ensure a proper balance of mood, tone, and key. (A Parry diary entry reads: 'After tea to-night was obliged to go to a music evening with Browning, and contrary to my expectation, I enjoyed myself very much.') Shrewdly, he left his library door open on these evenings, providing a refuge for boys who found an entire recital unduly demanding on the concentration.

Browning might have been expected to stay at Eton until his retirement. Unfortunately, he met his nemesis in the shape of the new Head Master, the Revd J. J. Hornby, O. E. (Head Master 1868-84, Provost 1884-1909). At a first glance, Hornby seems like a Titan among Head Masters. Within months of assuming the headmastership, he put in place a series of reforms, some dictated by the Public Schools Commission's recommendations, others (such as the abolition of the compulsory 3 o'clock Evensong on half-holidays) indirectly related to them. Under Hornby, the cult of athleticism flourished as never before at Eton whilst less manly pursuits were left to fend for themselves. Drama in all its forms was actively discouraged, as were the kind of musical events – 'the absurd mania for classical concerts and intellectual amusements for boys' – which Browning had worked so hard to establish.

In reality, Hornby was no Titan. He was a withdrawn, self-effacing man who spent the greater part of his time in the relative seclusion of his riverside villa. For sixteen long years, he ruled, if he ruled at all, through charm and charm alone. His successor but one, Edward Lyttelton, whose arrival as a boy at Eton coincided with Hornby's arrival as Head Master, would write:

The attempts made by a few progressives on the Staff to goad Hornby into further activities of administration were resisted with a courteous immobility to which educational history affords no parallel. No one of the masters had ever met anyone so imperturbably dignified or genial or so adamantine in his refusal to act. At first he gave audience to his voluble advisers; subsequently he requested them to put their views in writing. The epistles were duly acknowledged, but it is not in evidence that they were ever read. The time came when they ceased to be written.

Browning, it goes without saying, loathed Hornby and waged his own private war of attrition against 'that idiot of a person – the head, or rather tail, of Eton' as he somewhat tactlessly put it in a letter to his friend, the pianist and Wagnerian, Edward Dannreuther. This proved dangerous. Idle men rarely lack the energy to rid themselves of their tormentors and Hornby, for all his courtesy, was no exception to this rule. He was also, for all that he was a lax disciplinarian, something of a zealot in 'moral' matters. (Asked if a bust of Shelley could be placed in Upper School, he is said to have replied, 'No. He was a bad man'.)

Relationships with Browning reached an *impasse*, as such relationships often do, on a technicality when Browning attempted to take more pupils into his house than the statutes permitted.[1] Hornby, who had already challenged Browning on the issue of excessive 'familiarity' with certain pupils, saw his chance and dismissed him: without appeal and without compensation, either to Browning, or to his mother who had been his invaluable helper in running the house. Three of Eton's most distinguished masters – Francis Warre Cornish, H. E. Luxmoore and A. C. Ainger – offered to tender their resignations, but they were dissuaded. E. C. Austen Leigh was

1 The controversy reached the House of Commons where a motion was moved to draw up an amendment to the Public Schools Act. It had some supporters (the young A. J. Balfour among them) but was thrown out by the House.

less sanguine. Browning, he argued, had been 'insubordinate and unscrupulous'. But, then, like Hornby, Austen Leigh loathed music: or, rather, thought he did. A diary entry from 26 August, 1890 reads: 'I actually went to the Albert Hall and heard [Handel's] *Israel in Egypt* under Barnby's auspices and liked it!'

The scandal of Browning's dismissal was still resounding round Eton when the young M. R. James arrived there as a King's Scholar. Many years later, during his time as Provost, James made the brave but dubious claim that Eton had not been anti-arts in Hornby's time. 'Eton will not interfere with those who choose to walk the byways,' he argued, so long as it is not required to agree that 'the eccentric is the only right-minded person.' Did he have Oscar Browning in mind when he wrote those words? And who was it who wrote the superb obituary of Browning in the *Eton College Chronicle* with its reference to a kindly, active, egotistical life with its disappointing checks and frequent failures where duty was concerned?[2]

Browning attended the first performance of Wagner's complete *Ring* cycle at Bayreuth in 1876, one of the only Englishman not professionally associated with the event to do so. After his dismissal from Eton, he travelled the continent with George Curzon, one of the pupils whom Hornby (though not the boy's father) had accused him of corrupting.[3] He taught history at King's College, Cambridge and, after his retirement, spent much of his time in Rome. A friend who visited him there in 1920 wondered at the fact that he was still taking piano lessons at the age of 83.

2 *Eton College Chronicle*, 18 October, 1923.
3 Marquess Curzon of Kedleston (1859-1925). Viceroy of India (1898-1905), member of Lloyd George's war cabinet (1916-18), Foreign Secretary (1919-24)

Music remained his passion. Members of the Cambridge University Musical Society found they had acquired from Eton a most appreciative listener. Ensconced in his regular fireside seat, his legs barely touching the floor, he would declare most things 'awfully good'. As the *Westminster Gazette* reported after his death in 1923: 'There was nothing finnicking or hyper-sensitive or over-refined in Oscar Browning's attitude towards the noblest of arts'.

CHAPTER 9

Reform

Miss Hackett and Mr Barnby

The work of the Public Schools Commission had not gone unnoticed by the octogenarian Miss Maria Hackett. In 1868, she published a short but devastating indictment of Eton's betrayal of its musical past, *A Voice from the Tomb Seriously Addressed to all Etonians who Revere the Memory of the Founder.* The Commission report had interpreted the original statutes thus: 'To advance religion, a noble chapel was erected, where stated services were to be celebrated by an ample choir'. Miss Hackett glossed this in a footnote:

ETON COLLEGE as originally constituted by the Royal Founder may be regarded as the noblest MUSIC SCHOOL in the kingdom. From the highest to the lowest member of College no one can be statutably admitted to share in the revenues or benefits of the Foundation without musical talent or training. The youngest child who is a candidate for a place in the choir must be endowed with the rarely combined natural gifts of ear and voice; no youth can be statutably promoted to the Upper School as a KING'S SCHOLAR till he has mastered the preparatory course of liberal education, Music and Grammar.

The Commission's own recommendation was that a body of choristers be re-established for the exclusive use of the College chapel. This was better than nothing and Miss Hackett was pleased to do business with Eton's new Precentor, the Revd Leighton George Hayne, an Old Etonian with Schubertian spectacles and a Brahmsian beard, who was concerned to act on the principal reforms. By 1869 a blueprint had been drawn up for the engaging of twelve choristers with the option of four more. They were to be boarded with Dames, given instruction in Latin, French, Mathematics, Music and Divinity, and paid a stipend of between £15 and £25 a year depending on experience.

The plan soon ran into trouble. Hayne experienced difficulty in recruiting suitably qualified Lay Clerks. More seriously, there was stiff opposition from within Eton; not to the acquisition of choristers, the Commission required that, but to every other aspect of the scheme. The boarding idea was rejected, as was the plan to teach the choristers at Eton. As early as February 1868, Hayne had warned Miss Hackett, 'Their education will probably still be carried on at St Mark's, unless I can get a higher social class of boys, when a better education must be provided'. Not until Hornby retired as Provost some forty years later was the idea accepted of a choir school (of locally recruited day boys) within Eton's own precinct.

Hayne made some progress with the partly reformed choir. In March 1869, he was able to reassure Miss Hackett:

We have six lay clerks and four secondaries and a full Cathedral service is regularly performed every day throughout the year (irrespective of school term or holidays) at 4.30 p.m. On Sundays and Festivals, we also have a Cathedral service at 10.40 a.m.

He also began what advancing technology would turn into a fifty-year odyssey to equip College Chapel with a properly functioning organ suitable to its needs. An amateur organ-builder himself, he invited Hill & Son to reconstruct the existing organ and place it on a wooden screen at the west end of the building. The reconstruction was not a success. The heavy action made the organ extremely difficult to play and the screen itself was replaced within the decade.

In 1872 a search began for a successor to Hayne. When Oscar Browning got wind of the move, he wrote his friend George Grove for advice. Grove had a candidate in mind but wanted reassurance from Browning (who had no doubt regaled him with lurid tales of Hornby's unmusical nature) that Eton would be suitably welcoming:

> All I want to do is ensure him a favourable reception from you. I feel sure that he has more genius, more geniality, more tact, more power of teaching and attracting fellows, more practical gifts than any other musician I have ever met. I know that if any change in music is made at Eton, your knowledge of music, and weight in the College, will give you greater influence than anyone else.

Grove's candidate was a dazzling all-round talent by the name of Arthur Sullivan.[1] Since Sullivan and that witty young curmudgeon W. S. Gilbert had met but not yet embarked on their sequence of world-delighting operettas, we must be thankful that Sullivan did not become Precentor in 1872.

*

The number of applicants for the post was large. The successful candidate – the very model of a mid-Victorian public school musician – was Charles Maclean (1843-1916), a gifted Oxford-educated organist who had spent a number of years as a Civil Servant in Madras. Maclean introduced house singing

1 English engineer, self-taught writer and musicologist, Sir George Grove (1820-1900) was a close friend of Sullivan. During a memorable visit to Vienna in 1867, they unearthed Schubert's *Rosamunde* music. In 1873, Grove resigned his position with the Crystal Palace to edit what was to be his monument, his grand and authoritative *A Dictionary of Music and Musicians* (1st edition, London, 1879-89).

classes, engaged German 'professors' to teach solo instruments, and pioneered new initiatives of the town-and-gown variety; but after three years of coping with what he no doubt saw as a large and occasionally unruly tribe of aristocrats camped out beneath castle walls in the lower reaches of the River Thames, he returned to Madras where the natives, if not more friendly, were rather more susceptible to reform.[2]

Maclean was succeeded by the 37-year-old Yorkshire-born Joseph Barnby, a figure of some consequence in the world of Anglican church music and the first truly distinguished Eton Precentor of modern times. Barnby's appointment must have caused eyebrows to be raised in more conservative circles at Eton. His reputation was that of a musician fond of the grand gesture and a decidedly perfumed style of writing and performing. During his time as a London church organist, he had performed his own adaptation of Gounod's sumptuous and exciting *Messe solennelle de Sainte Cécile* at St Andrew's, Wells Street, a church more used to the severity of plainchant than harps and saccharine harmonies.[3] He had later caused even greater controversy during his time as organist and choir-master of St Anne's, Soho where he had at his disposal a choir of 37 trebles, 8 altos, 12 tenors, and 12 basses. Regular worshippers dubbed his Evensongs 'the Sunday operas' and expressed outrage at the behaviour of the cultural *arrivistes* who now flocked to St Anne's. During the anthem ('my

2 Maclean never entirely gave up his musical ambitions. In 1880 he was runner-up in a competition to find a new organist for the Crystal Palace and in 1892 he was a candidate for the position of Principal of the Guildhall School of Music. (The post went to Barnby.) A talented linguist who was fond of holidaying in Germany, he became acquainted in his later years with Richard Strauss.

3 Barnby was a friend of Gounod. They were co-founders of the Albert Hall Choral Society.

musical sermon' as Barnby called it) looks would be exchanged at some particularly felicitous piece of phrasing or vocal colour; necks would crane to identify a particular singer. The anthem over, the *arrivistes* departed *en masse*.

With or without Hornby's blessing, Barnby re-energised Eton's music. Music lessons were put on a more formal footing and Barnby's 'Sunday Evening Musical' became a popular weekly event. M. R. James recalled with pleasure performing music from Handel's *Messiah*, *Theodora*, and *Saul* (the magnificent opening sequence a life-long favourite) as well as Spohr's *Calvary* and Mendelssohn's *Elijah*. Concerts were staged in College Hall, including substantial extracts from Handel's *Acis and Galatea*, the work Arne's father had tried to plagiarise. James's only gripe was Barnby's addiction to contemporary music. Early in 1882, he fired off a letter of complaint to the *Eton College Chronicle* over the signature 'O Sapientia'. At a recent College Evensong Boyce's anthem 'O where shall wisdom be found' ('noblest of anthems') had been replaced at short notice by 'something or other by Mendelssohn'. Barnby replied in the following issue in the guise of 'Dixit Inspiens', 'a name at least as appropriate to your correspondent as to myself'. O Sapientia, he averred, was clearly ignorant of the fact that illness and absence often necessitated last-minute adjustments to a choir's published programme. As for 'something or other by Mendelssohn':

… I must content myself with merely pointing out that, in respect of excellence as a composer, Mendelssohn has been generally held to possess a certain superiority over this Doctor Boyce; I may remark, in passing, on this particular anthem, 'O where shall wisdom be found', that it is a good specimen of that solid old class of cathedral anthem which the compositions of Gounod, Hiller, Sullivan, and a few other modern masters, to a great extent superseded. The best possible contrast I can think of, between the two schools of composers, is that afforded by a comparison of Gounod's 'Here by Babylon's Wave' with Boyce's 'By the waters of Babylon', an anthem which would, I doubt not, exactly suit your correspondent's taste.

The curious aspect of this exchange is that it is the 19-year-old King's Scholar who is the conservative (James's antiquarian interests already shining through), the 43-year-old Precentor who is the unrepentant modernist.

Edward Lyttelton, who returned to Eton as a master in 1882, found Barnby more interested in staging grand events (a semi-professional performance of Mendelssohn's *Elijah*, for example, with the incomparable Charles Santley as one of the soloists) than trying to convert the bawling mass of Etonians into tolerable singers. In the summer of 1888, during a brief indisposition, Barnby asked Lyttelton – a keen amateur singer with a passionate belief in the educative power of choral work – if he would take over rehearsal of the Musical Society. Lyttelton was thrilled. He had never conducted but, like many amateur music-lovers, harboured a deep-down desire to do so. He had at his disposal a choir of over two hundred voices – 70 trebles, 50 altos, 45 tenors, 70 basses – which even Joah Bates might been pleased to marshal. He recalled:

The effect was grand. I have known exhilarating moments in life, especially the opening of a run with the foxhounds on a fine day, and the sensation on a high glacier in the Alps at 3 a.m. on a bright moonlight night with congenial companions; but for the kind of co-operative joy which causes a real forgetfulness of self, give me the conducting of a chorus of high-spirited youngsters sufficiently drilled to follow the beat with real attention, and with really good music to sing.

Lyttelton's elegantly written autobiography *Memories and Hopes* was published in 1925 by which time Eton had, indeed, begun to establish a school-based choral tradition of some note.[4]

★

One problem Barnby needed to address was the state of the organ in College Chapel. His opportunity came in 1882 when a new stone screen was erected at the west end of the chapel (driven into the Wall Paintings on either side, a matter of no concern, it seems, to the Provost and Fellows) in memory of Eton Officers who had lost their lives in the Afghan, Zulu and Transvaal wars of 1879-81. Since the organ had to be dismantled, it was sent for extensive overhaul to Hill's workshops where it was destroyed in a fire on 7 October, 1882. Like the destruction of the chapel's Victorian stained-glass windows by a German bomb in 1940, this was a misfortune over which there was a certain amount of private rejoicing. Delays to the replacement were the subject of a certain amount of snide comment in the *Eton College Chronicle* but Barnby eventually opened the new organ, to no particular fanfares from the College authorities, at Evensong on the Fourth of June, 1885.

The case, designed by J. L. Pearson and painted by Clayton & Bell (the painting paid for by the Vice-Provost, the Revd

4 A list provided by Mr Nigel Jaques of choral works he performed in during his time as a boy at Eton (1948-54) shows how wide-ranging and esoteric the repertory eventually became : Handel *Messiah*, Haydn *The Seasons* ('Spring'), Dyson *The Canterbury Pilgrims*, Holst *Christmas Day*, Bach *St John Passion*, Purcell *King Arthur*, Brahms *Liebeslieder Waltzes*, Bach *St Matthew Passion*, Balfour Gardiner *News from Whydah*, Purcell *Dioclesian*, Haydn *The Seasons* ('Winter'), Stanford *The Revenge*, Parry *At a Solemn Music: Blest Pair of Sirens*, Vaughan Williams *In Windsor Forest*, Handel *L'allegro, Il penseroso*.

John Wilder) is one of the finest of its period, a superb example of High Victorian decorative art. Unfortunately, neither the hydraulic system of blowing nor the later 'Otto' gas system was satisfactory. The organ was rebuilt in 1902 incorporating tubular pneumatic blowing but only became fully effective when electrical blowing equipment was installed in 1922.[5]

*

Eton must have seemed the perfect stepping-off point for Barnby. In fact, he held the post of Precentor until 1892. Clearly, there were times when he had his misgivings. Meeting Oscar Browning in London in 1882, he remarked, 'I am just beginning to learn what sort of place Eton is'. To which Browning is said to have replied, 'And I am just beginning to forget'.

The fact that Barnby was allowed to pursue his flourishing career as a choral conductor outside Eton was evidently a factor in the College retaining his services. Shortly after he arrived at Eton, Barnby had been obliged to take over performances of Verdi's new *Messa da Requiem* at the Royal Albert Hall after Verdi had returned to Italy angered by the mixture of indifference and disapproval with which the work had been received. Not that it was all plain sailing for Barnby. Schoolmasters are not normally used to having their work reviewed in the press or the reviews read by their pupils. Towards the end of his time at Eton, Barnby was on the receiving end of some particularly withering notices from that most

5 Further changes were made in 1925-7, funded in part by John Christie (see p.156). The organ was restored in 1987 by N. P. Mander, Ltd and the pipe fronts repainted by Plowden & Smith, Ltd.

entertaining scourge of the late-Victorian London musical scene, George Bernard Shaw. Barnby was said to have turned Handel's *Messiah* into a 'dull, lumbering, heavy-footed choral monster'. When, shortly after leaving Eton, he enterprisingly tried conclusions with a public performance of Berlioz's *La damnation de Faust*, Shaw wrote:

To comb that wild composer's hair, stuff him into a frock-coat and tall hat, stick a hymn-book in his hand, and obtain reverent applause for his ribald burlesque of an Amen chorus as if it were a genuine Handelian solemnity, is really a remarkable feat, and one which few conductors except Sir Joseph Barnby could achieve.

But Shaw also praised Barnby. In May 1892, he acknowledged the degree to which Barnby had helped transform standards of choral singing in England in the past fifteen years. Writing after a performance of Mendelssohn's *Elijah*, he observed:

There was no screaming from the sopranos, no bawling from the tenors, no growling from the basses. By dispensing with these three staple ingredients of English choral singing Mr Barnby has achieved a triumph...

He also admired Barnby's presentation of the London première of Dvořák's *Requiem*, whilst being amazed that 'any critic should mistake this paltry piece of orchestral and harmonic confectionery for a serious composition.' In the summer of 1893, Shaw summed up in a sentence the uphill struggle music still faced in Victorian England:

On Saturday evening the Lord Mayor of London invited me to the Mansion House to meet about three hundred and forty representatives of Art and Literature. Music, the art for which England was once famous throughout Europe, was represented by the police band, Mr Ganz, Mr Kuhe, Sir Joseph Barnby, and myself.

Barnby's compositional legacy to Eton includes a number of songs he wrote in collaboration with the local poetaster, A. C. Ainger. Pieces such as *The Silver Thames* and *Cricket is King* have fallen into decent obscurity but two songs continue to be sung. *Carmen Etonense* is an A minor march (shades of Mahler's Sixth Symphony) with a Trio in the major whose visceral top F sharp has a touch of savagery about it which will always catch non-Etonians unawares. The second song, *Time ever flowing*, is a kind of arrested Tchaikovskian waltz-song in Barnby's own most characteristic style, rather tamer than *Carmen Etonense* but pleasing enough in its way.

Among the music chosen by Barnby for his funeral, which took place at St Paul's Cathedral on 4 February, 1896, was Mendelssohn's 'Happy and blest are those that have endured', an anthem which could reasonably be sung at any school-master's funeral.

CHAPTER 10

Eton's Wagnerians

Oscar Browning, H. E. Luxmoore
and John Christie

When Oscar Browning arrived in Bayreuth in the summer of
1876 to attend the first complete performance of Wagner's
Ring, he tried, with his usual bullish enthusiasm, to gain access
to a rehearsal. He was turned away. Even Brahms, he was
informed, had been refused that privilege. (Brahms was not
even in Bayreuth.) Sitting in Wagner's new Festival Theatre
watching *The Ring*, Browning decided that his dismissal by
Hornby had been more a privilege than a disgrace. He even
wrote a letter to *The Times* (how Hornby must have smiled)
bidding 'English lovers of music not to neglect an opportunity
of hearing the perfect execution of a work of art such as will
not occur again in the present generation'.

The following year, Browning received an invitation from
Mrs Dannreuther which he must have clutched at:

Will you come in on Thursday evening to meet the Meister? He promises
to read his new work, *Parsival*, to us at 8.30, so do not come late please.

For all this, Browning was never the perfect Wagnerite. As the
years passed, only *Die Meistersinger* held him more or less
permanently in thrall. In his own private pantheon, Mozart,
Pergolesi, and Rossini continued to hold pride of place.

*

The youngest of the trio of now legendary Eton masters from
this time – and the only one not to be sacked – was H. E.

Luxmoore. He first visited Bayreuth in 1898 in the company of Cecil Spring-Rice. He was equivocal about *Parsifal*. After seeing it for a second time, he wrote to Edward Lyttelton:

Parsifal himself is such a very partial ideal, & Gurnemanz is very near being a bore... but it takes the gamut of Heaven & Hell & as most of us are somewhere between one can't escape. it is awfully big & griping [*sic*].

He also saw *The Ring*:

... of course there are long foggy things for an outsider – but these new myths take hold of me, & there are goodly bits of humour, & glorious exciting tunes & things really beautiful like the Rhine maidens & Siegfried forging the sword &c.

During Luxmoore's second visit, in 1900, *Lohengrin* was on the programme. He was mesmerised by the Prelude – 'I shall never forget my first introduction to the heavenly shimmering of the violins in the introduction' – but worried by the fact that the only men capable of singing the title role appeared to be overweight effeminate poseurs. He added:

I don't believe that Wagner is the greatest musician, but I do think he is one the greatest theatrical contrivers, & that his use of stage effect, patriotic legend, poetical situations & music that is often weirdly and pungently pathetic & sometimes magnificently great makes him more attractive to outsiders than the pure musician.

*

Eton's most passionate Wagnerite, a man who would go on to found an opera festival of his own, though not one given over, as he ideally would have wished, to the works of the master, was John Christie (1882-1962).

The only son of Augustus Christie, a wealthy but mentally

deranged country squire, and Lady Rosamond Christie, the third daughter of the fifth Earl of Portsmouth, he inherited his father's astonishing physical robustness, as well as a certain bellicose eccentricity that, happily, stopped short of certifiable lunacy. He had a troubled childhood, not least because he was the vessel into which his mother's affections were more or less exclusively poured. Having survived a particularly brutal Prep School, he entered Eton in January 1896. He was well-placed academically though his school career was to be unremarkable in everything except science, itself very much a Cinderella subject in English public schools at the time.

After a year in the military, he was lamed for life in a riding accident. He blamed himself for the accident but took issue with 'criminally incompetent Army doctors' for leaving his foot unexamined for ten days. It was this which eventually took him back to Eton where he taught science in new but chronically underfunded Science Schools to which he made a more than generous donation.

Christie's two passions in these years were motor cars, which he endlessly stripped and rebuilt and which he drove with a ferocity Mr Toad himself might have admired, and Wagner. As Luxmoore had observed, Wagner's most fanatical adherents were to be found as much among non-musicians as musicians. Christie made a point of seeing and hearing just about everything London had to offer the fervent Wagnerian. He even took his grandfather to a Wagner evening at the Queen's Hall. 'Music is not very much in his line,' he wrote to his mother. 'However, he did not talk.'

This obsession with Wagner and cars reached its climax in 1904 when Christie organised what must be counted the most extraordinary expedition to Bayreuth ever to leave these shores. The trip involved Charles Harford Lloyd, Barnby's successor as Precentor, with whom Christie shared a passion for church organs, George Lyttelton,[1] R. H. Longman, and Christie himself. Since Christie's Georges-Richard was an open two-seater and since luggage and petrol needed to be carried, he was obliged to attach a trailer to the motor, a crate on wheels which had originally been designed for transporting cheese.

Getting across the Channel was a potential problem which Christie overcame by hiring a barge which was attached to the back of cross-Channel steamer. The journey from the French coast to Bayreuth was long and dusty and the car frequently overheated. (When water was not immediately to hand, the contents of the passengers' bladders were called on instead). The party duly arrived in Bayreuth where they heard *Tannhäuser, Tristan and Isolde* and *The Ring*. They also heard the last two acts of *Parsifal*, the car having failed to get them into town in time for the scheduled start.

*

Returning to Eton as a master, Christie settled into the bachelor colony at 2, Common Lane, shortly to be dubbed 'Liqueur Cottage' on account of the encyclopaedic array of liqueurs on the dining-room sideboard. Christie struck up close friendships with G. W. ('Tuppy') Headlam, a caustic, able man, and the scholar and athlete C. M. Wells. It proved to be an agreeable fellowship: Wells taught Christie about wine, Christie taught Wells how to fish.

The inhabitants of Liqueur Cottage were not universally

1 The Hon. George W. Lyttelton (1883-1962), Eton 1895-1901, Master 1908-45, joint author of the celebrated correspondence with Rupert Hart-Davis.

loved by their colleagues. A monied lifestyle which revolved around operas, fine wines, and expensive motors caused eyebrows to be raised even then, even in Eton. It did not help that Christie was a law unto himself. At the age of 24, he thought nothing of calling boys by their Christian names, an unheard of act of familiarity. His science teaching was disorganised but enthusiastic; his Maths teaching was hopeless. After the First World War, he became even more remiss. It was not unusual for early morning divisions to be received by his manservant, Childs, with the announcement that Captain Christie had overslept but should be expected shortly.

*

Christie's war record had, needless to say, been extraordinary. Blind in one eye (an accident with a cricket ball), lame, and well into this thirties, he was determined to win a commission and succeeded in joining the 9th Battalion, King's Royal Rifles in October 1914. He served in Flanders between June and December 1915 after which he was recalled to England and retired from active service on medical grounds.

During his months in the trenches, he wrote numerous letters to his mother, who unbeknown to him was plotting in high places to have him recalled from active service, to his uncle, Vernon Watney, and to 'Tuppy' Headlam back in Eton. In the introduction to his annotated edition of the Headlam letters, Andrew Robinson observes:

Matter-of-fact about the horrors of war – discovering two lumps in Ypres which transpire to be gravely wounded but still living servicemen, crawling back to his line under fire, dragging a man with two broken legs – Christie saw things of which he can scarcely have dreamed during his days as a schoolmaster, dazzled then by twentieth-century technology ('Christie the motorist' A. C. Benson notes him in his diary). Something of this comes in his dispassionate interest in the composition of poison gases, of liquid fire, of mortars and the thrills to be derived from flying over an anti-aircraft battery. At the same time, his requests for a supply of soap, spare shirts, a folding arm-chair, Tiptree jam, fishing waders and the latest results from the Eton Field Game... come as jolt to those who see the First World War in monochrome.[2]

The letters are, indeed, remarkable:

Body brought along and then read the Burial service over him. This description may sound callous but I was really rather distressed by the fellow being killed. He had just opened a 2 inch loop hole and within a few seconds a bullet came through below the eye and out the back of his head. He was unconscious for a few minutes, then died. It's all part of the job. Pretty bloody, isn't it? [13.vi.1915]

Sitting at tea outside, and hun getting louder and nearer. Flash and bang and clump singing over our heads. I lay flat and upset the jam. [ibid.]

Tuppy, this war is too bloody for words. [ibid.]

Glorious morning. Small breakfast. Felt very well. Remember 3 or 4 years ago. Poured all day on Thursday at Eton. Very little at Lord's. Friday and Saturday very hot. Hard wicket, much surprised at the time. Never thought I should be doing this. Spirits very high this morning. Now drizzling; spirits lower. The ground is saturated with the gas from the gas shells of the last few weeks. Curious rain seems to bring it out. Supposed to be dibrinoxylene (Check!) [Dibromoxylene]. Don't know much about it. Hurts the eyes – men all watering at the eyes badly, crying. Motor goggles help. [15.vii.1915]

2 The Letters of Captain John Christie, 9th Bttn KRRC 42nd Inf Brigade 14th Division BEF to G. 'Tuppy' Headlam, June-December, 1915, Eton School Library MSS, ed. A. S. Robinson, 1994, unpublished.

Charles Murray is killed. It was quite the most beastly day we've had.[3] [27.ix.1915]

Pheasants for lunch. Have seen them cooking and they look to be nearly done. Bread crumbs lost with the kit. [12.x.1915]

Will Lewis please send out twice the quantity of game. Going to fly over our area shortly I hope. Must arrange to be shelled then. They never hit you and it would be a new experience. Had no incidents with shells lately. Was shot at looking over the trench the other day. Bullet went into the sandbag just in front of my face. Fortunately about 6 inches too low. [11.xii.1915]

By such slender margins do the fates of great institutions hang. Two months earlier, another restless, pioneering, self-willed eccentric, Lieutenant John Reith, had come within millimetres of death when a bullet shattered his right cheekbone during the Battle of Loos. Now Christie had avoided a similar fate by a similarly narrow margin. The fact that Reith lived to shape the BBC into the world-revered institution it quickly became and that Christie lived to found Glyndebourne, a more modest but no less exemplary institution, causes one to wonder what civilisation was denied by the deaths of those members of this astonishing generation who did not survive.

When Christie's men were pinned down hour after hour by heavy bombardment, he read them extracts from Spenser's *The Faerie Queen*, Plato's dialogues, and *Alice through the Looking-Glass*. Since he reports in one of his letters that his men appear to say nothing but 'fuck', one wonders what they made of this. Reith planned the BBC on a not dissimilar premise, 'I know precisely what the great British people want, and they're damn well not going to get it'.

3 Aged 19. His obituary in the *Eton College Chronicle* on 7 October, 1915 noted: 'though he was a quiet and gentle boy, never was there one who radiated from his whole being such simplicity and unselfishness'.

Christie left Eton in 1922 aged 40 to attend to the family estates. It has been said that the forties is the decade in a man's life when energy and experience sit in the happiest conjunction. Certainly, it was not long before Christie was embarking on the venture for which he is best remembered, the founding of the Glyndebourne Opera. He was greatly helped in the venture by the Mounseys: Johnnie Mounsey, a director of Barclays Bank, and his wife, Fanny. It was Fanny, in particular, who steered Christie in the direction of Mozart, away from his beloved Wagner.

The earliest performances took place in 1928-9 with audiences drawn from estate workers, tenants, house guests, and any locals who cared to turn up. Christie played Antonio the gardener in a performance of Act 2 of Mozart's *Le nozze di Figaro* and Beckmesser in a performance of the start of Act 3 of Wagner's *Die Meistersinger*. He was no singer and had a fallible sense of rhythm but, assiduously coached by Fanny Mounsey, his Beckmesser was accounted a triumph. It is, of course, one of the funniest episodes in all opera as Beckmesser limps in from his recent beating and, finding Sachs's shop unoccupied, starts rummaging around in search of the prize-song. Still, it says much for Christie's performance that a housemaid had to be carried out in hysterics.

In 1930, after Johnnie Mounsey's death and a period of great gloom at Glyndebourne, Christie engaged the 29-year-old Audrey Mildmay to sing Blonde in Act 1 of Mozart's *Die Entführung aus dem Serail*. It is said that while Christie was showing her over the house, he opened a door and announced 'This is where we shall sleep when we are married'. True or not, they were married the following year on that most Etonian of dates, the Fourth of June. Marriage to Audrey helped put paid once and for all to the idea of a festival based on Wagner rather than on Mozart, though Christie himself was reluctant to let the idea go. He was once heard discussing where best to place the bells in *Parsifal* as producer Carl Ebert gazed anxiously about him at the theatre's modest facilities.

Nowadays, Glyndebourne is often said to be 'elitist', not least because of its dress code. Christie insisted on his audience wearing evening dress 'out of respect for our work'. He had a passion for quality (if that is elitism, so be it) but he was no snob. His principal concerns were the opera's solvency and the state of the buildings. He was particularly obsessed with the design and functioning of the lavatories and, like many a thrifty gentleman of mature years, spent a great deal of time going round switching off lights.

He never forgot Eton. As an old man, he talked a good deal about the 'great' memories such as the match at Lord's in 1911 when Fowler's 8 for 23 saved Eton from certain defeat.

The 1939 Glyndebourne season ended on 15 July with a performance of *Così fan tutte*. When Christie appeared on stage at the end with some 'serious news', the audience was apprehensive. The news? Eton had lost to Harrow at Lord's: the school's first defeat at the hands of the old enemy since 1908.

CHAPTER II

Land of Hope and Glory

Benson, Elgar and Clara Butt

Arthur Benson, the writer and revered Eton schoolmaster who provided the text for Edward Elgar's *Coronation Ode* from which 'Land of Hope and Glory' derives, was the second son of E. W. Benson. A schoolmaster himself, Edward Benson had been selected at the age of 29 to be the first Master of Wellington College, the Prince Consort's brainchild, before going on to become Bishop of Truro in 1877[1] and, in 1883, Archbishop of Canterbury. Edward's marriage into the family of his close relations, the intellectually brilliant Sidgwicks, was to create one of the most influential, though also one of the most emotionally troubled late-Victorian academic dynasties. Arthur was particularly affected. The inheritor of his father's predisposition to clinical depression, he also shared his mother's homoerotic needs. The depressions, which had begun at an early age, had engendered in him a sense that, for all his manifest gifts and powers, he was somehow a failure. It was this, above all, which caused him to resist attempts to foist the Eton headmastership upon him in 1905.

Arthur and his youngest brother, Hugh, had both been educated at Eton,[2] but it was Arthur who was to make the

---

1 Another inaugural occupancy. While at Truro, Edward Benson introduced a Christmas service which closely resembles the Festival of Nine Lessons and Carols which King's College, Cambridge introduced in 1918. Though the King's service, including the magnificent Bidding Prayer, was written by the Dean, Eric Milner-White, Arthur Benson may well have been the conduit for the idea.

2 The eldest son, Martin, who died of meningitis whilst at school, was a scholar at Winchester; Fred, the novelist E. F. Benson, had been sent to Marlborough.

most of the school and its ambient world. As David Newsome notes in his superb biography of Benson, *On the Edge of Paradise*, Benson's career placed him at various stages of his life within the most eminent and influential circles of contemporary England:

There was the ecclesiastical circle that centred upon Lambeth, in many ways his natural and domestic milieu, not only because he was his father's son but also because of his enduring friendship with Archbishop Randall Davidson. There were the propinquent circles of Eton College and Windsor Castle, in both of which Arthur found a place – as of right and natural inclination at Eton, where he had been King's Scholar, master and housemaster, and by chance or good fortune at Windsor, through his remarkable facility in producing hymns, odes and verses for special occasions which elevated him for a while to the position of a sort of unofficial poet laureate.

Commissions had, indeed, come thick and fast from the Castle after Benson's success in pressing into service for the wedding of two minor royals a hymn he had already written for the wedding of an Eton friend. Queen Victoria herself would later set one of his hymns to music, Princess Beatrice another.

It helped that Benson got on famously with the new Master of the Queen's Musick, Walter Parratt. Hitherto, Benson had found musicians a 'hard lot': 'Their minds seem to be enclosed in a small park. They are without humanity, absorbed, fond of details, fond of bad jokes, desultory, apt to consider small things important'. Parratt, though, had a charm, high-mindedness, and breadth of view which entirely captivated Benson.

Along with Eton's new Precentor, Charles Lloyd, Benson would often watch royal gatherings from the relative safety of the St George's organ-loft. 'Relative safety' because on one occasion amusement at the antics of a nervous cellist in the chapel below turned to dismay as a plumed bonnet bobbed into view on the organ-loft stairs. It was the Queen. Benson managed to hide behind the choir-organ from where he was able to observe Lloyd 'with fear written in every feature, bowing wildly from the waist in all directions'.

Benson was formally presented to Queen Victoria in May 1899 during the annual Eton and Windsor madrigal concert at Windsor. The Queen did not always attend the event. The previous year, Princess Christian had presided, unamused at the antics of Hubert Parry. Benson, whose verses 'Home of my heart' had been movingly set by Parry,[3] recorded the scene in his diary:

> Parry conducted his own songs. He blew on the pitch pipe, which was first silent and then emitted a groan. He said, in a silence between laughter, 'I knew I couldn't get the right note out of the beastly thing – Here, Lloyd!' and threw it twenty feet over the singers to Lloyd who missed it: it hit the wall and fell on the ground. Lloyd burrowed, roars of laughter. Princess Christian looked shocked. At last the right note was produced. When the thing was over P. Xtian swept out, but turned to bow to Parry, who stood with his back to her, talking loudly and mopping his brow. 'Look at that,' said Lady Parratt to me, 'Sir Hubert is no *courtier*', with bitter emphasis.

★

The death of Queen Victoria in January 1901 meant that there was a coronation toward. Benson sketched out words for a coronation ode and forwarded them to Parratt. The idea was accepted and the country's 'leading' composer, Charles Villiers Stanford, given first refusal. Stanford did refuse (and was then furious when nothing else came his way at coronation time).

3 *Eight Four-part Songs*, iv, 1898. The settings are dedicated to Walter Parratt.

Parratt now forwarded Benson's idea to Edward Elgar, English music's newest and brightest hope: 'Should it take your fancy [Benson] would be honoured & I most grateful if you could set it to immortal music'. Elgar accepted the commission.

In general, Benson's verses suited Elgar's purposes. He makes much of the opening 'Crown the King' with its movingly reflective central stanzas, and brings an undertow of menace to the Boer War section where Benson's writing is only patchily effective:

> Under the drifting smoke, and the scream of the flying shell,
> When the hillside hisses with death, – and never a foe in sight

Curiously, the one sequence Elgar either did not warm to, or lacked the time to seek out inspiration, was Benson's intended tribute to the arts, fair nurse of peace, in the section beginning 'Hark, Upon the Hallowed Air'.

The most famous lines in the Coronation Ode, 'Land of Hope and Glory, Mother of the free', did not appear in Benson's original draft. In a letter to the singer Clara Butt in November 1927, Elgar recalled that it was the King himself who had suggested that the Ode be crowned with a vocal setting of the Trio from *Pomp and Circumstance* March No.1. Dame Clara disagreed most emphatically:

While listening to the tune in Pomp & Circumstance, I asked you to write something like it for me & after a little talk & persuasion on my part you said 'You shall have that one my dear'.[4]

Whoever dreamed up the idea, it caused consternation at

4 Undated letter, probably written in response to the letter of 21 November, 1927. Elgar had made a separate version of 'Land of Hope and Glory' for contralto, chorus, and orchestra which Clara Butt unveiled at a 'Coronation Concert' in the Royal Albert Hall in June 1902, before the King's illness.

Novello where the Publishing Manager, A. J. Jaeger ('Nimrod' in the *Enigma Variations*), attempted to show that the tune was unsingable when words were added to it. Elgar disagreed and asked Benson for more text, but Benson was none too happy either; he was worried by the music's metre. Finding himself in somewhat deeper water than he had anticipated when he first drafted the ode, he asked Elgar to string together a sample text – nonsense words if necessary – to give him the feel of the thing verbally. The famous opening lines came within the week, the rest following in the course of a detailed correspondence.

Work on the *Ode* was drawing to a close when Elgar received an urgent letter from Benson. During the course of a 'lonely walk' in the Sussex countryside, he had been struck by the appalling thought that the work made no reference to Queen Alexandra. Benson repaired the omission by making reference to her Danish origins, a passage set with great tenderness and warmth by Elgar, though only after he had tested Benson's patience to the limit by requesting numerous small changes to the wording.

The *Ode* was to have been unveiled at a state gala at Covent Garden on 24 June, 1902 in the presence of the entire court. Since there were no complimentary tickets to be had Elgar was obliged to pay a hefty 20 guineas apiece for seats for his wife and Benson. In the event, the king's appendicitis caused the eleventh-hour postponement of both gala and coronation. After the work's successful launch in Sheffield and London in October 1902, Elgar wrote to Benson: 'I did not intend the thing to lie on the musical antiquary's shelves, but wanted the 'people' – in the best sense of the word – to enjoy themselves: – and they are doing so'.

The royalties earned by 'Land of Hope and Glory' were substantial, leaving the publishers, Boosey & Hawkes, greedy for more. That same year, Benson provided Elgar with texts for two songs. *In the Dawn* chronicles the secret understanding that love brings. To have loved puts the soul 'among the stars'. *Speak, Music* expresses a longing for 'all that the poet, the priest cannot say'. Elgar told Benson he preferred the latter; others may disagree. A third song, *Speak, my Heart* (1903-4), also has words by Benson. It is a parody of a song of country wooing which Elgar had set to music only to find that his publishers were unable to clear the copyright on the original text by Arthur Ropes (or 'Adrian Ross' as he understandably preferred to call himself).

More astonishingly, Boosey & Hawkes tried to interest Benson in writing an opera libretto for Elgar, Cleopatra a possible subject. Benson noted in his diary that he had been assured it 'would be highly lucrative, & that I can well believe' but he had no expertise in this area and was, in any case, suffering from depression.

Benson continued to keep in touch with Elgar and attend performances of his music, though Elgar often seemed as depressed as Benson. After hearing *The Kingdom* in the chapel of King's College, Cambridge in June 1907, Benson wrote in his diary:

He told me his eyes were overstrained & he cd do no work - then he said simply that it was no sort of pleasure to him to hear *The Kingdom*, because it was so far behind what he had dreamed of – it only caused him shame & sorrow... He seemed all strung on wires, & confessed that he petitioned for a seat close to the door, that he might rush out if overcome...

Benson claimed he was 'no good at serious music', citing a performance of Bach's *B Minor Mass* in King's College Chapel which had bored him, but he liked *The Kingdom*: 'the music of Heaven, with a strange and unearthly quality about it'.

This was a momentous year for Elgar, for it was now that he resolved to abandon the idea of a trilogy of oratorios and confront instead the supreme challenge of a symphony, music unhampered by 'any poetic or literary basis'. He began work on his First Symphony in Rome in December 1907. Benson dined with him on 30 December and afterwards recorded in his diary a revealing image of Elgar's physical state whilst in the throes of composition:

E. in dress clothes – we were not – came eagerly out to fetch us in... He looked well, with his pale face, high-bridged nose, quick movements. But he said his eyes were weak & he cd. only work an hour a day. With all his pleasantness & some savoir faire, one feels instinctively that he is socially always a little uneasy – he has got none of Parratt's courtesy or Parry's geniality... Lady E. very kind but without charm & wholly conventional, though pathetically anxious to be *au courant* with a situation... E. lighted us down long stairs. The worst thing about him is the limp shake of his thin hand, wh. gives a feeling of great want of stamina.

★

The *Coronation Ode* was revived in 1911 for the coronation of George V and Queen Mary. Fresh verses were provided by Benson for the new queen whom he described as 'True Queen of English Hearts', a phrase which would be revived later in the century to describe another, very different queen-in-waiting.

By the time of the outbreak of war in 1914, 'Land of Hope and Glory' had virtually become a second national anthem.

Already there were voices raised against the piece, accusing it of jingoism. In fact, the poem contains some surprising lines, indicative of Benson's and Elgar's prophetic melancholy:

> Tho' thy way be darkened, still in splendour drest,
> As the star that trembles o'er the liquid West.
> Throned amid the billows, throned inviolate,
> Thou has reigned victorious, thou hast smiled at fate.

Roused now by the imminence of war, Elgar – who had done his bit by enrolling as a special constable in Hampstead – suggested to Benson that some new words might be appropriate in the new situation. For example:

> Leap thou then to battle,
> Bid thy hosts increase;
> Stand for faith & honour,
> Smite for truth & peace.

Benson responded and a correspondence ensued in which Elgar suggested as a possible model the American writer John Hay's *The Vengeance is God's*.

> How shall His vengeance be done?
> How, when His purpose is clear?
> Must He come down from His throne?
> Hath He no instrument here?

Benson was fairly appalled by this:

I'll turn to again, today or tomorrow & see if I can do anything – but I'm not strong in the *Vengeance* line, & indeed I don't see what there is to revenge as yet – we have hemmed in Germany tight all round for years, in the Goodnatured unsympathetic way in which Anglo-Saxons *do* treat the world, & the cork has flown out! I haven't the faintest doubt that the patriots in Germany are saying 'How long, O God, how long?' with *precisely* the same fervour & spontaneity.

The two stanzas Benson produced are more concerned with the flinging down of gauntlets than outright hostility. Indeed, the octet of the opening stanza as Benson originally drafted it is almost conciliatory:

> Dear Land of Hope, our joy & pride
> The crown upon thy brows is set
> Thy keen-eyed navies span the tide
> Thou hast been strong, be stronger yet!
> 'Tis not thy wont to rage and tear
> The crowns from other brows than thine
> And if thy comrades shine as fair
> Though dost not grudge to see them shine

The task was eventually completed and the new verses published in *The Times*. How often they were used is impossible to ascertain. Rather little, one suspects: and rarely, if ever, after 1918.

⋆

Dame Clara Butt, as she became in 1920 in recognition of her wartime charity work, sent her eldest son to Eton and so became a regular visitor to the school, a connection she and her husband, the baritone Kennerley Rumford, celebrated with a concert in School Hall in aid of the Eton Mission in July 1923.[5] Dame Clara was known for the exceptional power and range of her voice. (As one wag put it, the Royal Albert Hall must have been built in intelligent anticipation of her arrival.) In the course of an enthusiastic review of the concert, the *Eton College Chronicle* paid tribute to the voice's fabled power:

5 Mindful of the boys' eyes as well as their ears, the Kennerley Rumfords shared the platform with the young and beautiful Joan Carr (the future Lady Drogheda) who played three pieces by Chopin.

Dame Clara Butt held us spellbound with her singing. Even in the *Song of Nations*, when the audience joined in the chorus, her magnificent voice was heard far above the rest. We liked *A fairy went a-marketing* best of the songs and indeed it was encored. The concert was, as the Head Master said afterwards, like the Winchester match, 'a glorious draw'.

The cricketing analogy was apt. At the end of the concert, the Eton XI, of which Roy Kennerley Rumford was a member, processed towards the stage where they presented Dame Clara with a bouquet and her husband with a bat bound in blue Eton ribbon.

What is curious about the review is its failure to name the composer of the two items singled out for special praise. The composer's name was Arthur Goodhart. Since Goodhart had been an Eton master for the best part of 35 years, and before that a boy at Eton, this would seem to be confirmation of the ancient saw 'a prophet is not without honour, save in his own country'. Goodhart wrote a number of pieces for Dame Clara, including his ballad *The Island* and the aforementioned *Song of Nations*, commissioned to honour the founding of The League of Nations and premiered in the Royal Albert Hall with Dame Clara as soloist.

A recent Eton history describes Goodhart as 'a fussy, ineffective man but a respectable minor composer'. The latter point is true,[6] though it is difficult to see how a man who was variously Master-in-College, A. C. Benson's successor in Godolphin House, a competent teacher, and a distinguished play producer (his production of Marlowe's *Dr Faustus* was

6 Goodhart wrote and had published a set of orchestral variations on 'Tipperary', a Service in B flat, numerous songs, choral ballads, and anthems, and a number of piano and organ pieces, including an 'Introduction and Fugue' which C. V. Stanford

talked about for years afterwards) could be said to be 'ineffective'. Goodhart was George Butterworth's housemaster and, in later years, Anthony Powell's. If he was the model for Le Bas, the housemaster and failed poet in *A Dance to the Music of Time*, perhaps he was a bit of an oddity personally. 'At the time … he merely seemed to Stringham and myself to be a dangerous lunatic, to be humoured and outwitted.' But, then, what housemaster isn't so in the eyes of his more cynical charges?

Dame Clara's association with Eton came to an unhappy conclusion. Immediately after the Eton concert, her son made his second appearance for Eton against Harrow at Lord's, took part in a cricket week organised by J. M. Barrie, then attended an army camp from which he returned complaining of severe headaches. It was meningitis, and proved fatal. Dame Clara, a Christian Scientist, gave the public no glimpse of her distress and steadfastly embarked on a tour of Canada and the United States a few weeks later.

approved. Goodhart's Founder's Day cantata *England Stands for Honour* 'Dedicated to Lord Roberts and the Etonians serving under him in South Africa', quotes from a fifteenth-century carol, 'Alma Redemptoris Mater', several school songs and the sound of the chimes on Lupton's Tower. His unpublished work includes a short Wagner parody, 'The House that Jack Built', written for St George's School, Windsor in 1902. As concert programmes reveal, he was also a great admirer of Gilbert and Sullivan (see p. 144).

CHAPTER 12

The Lloyd years

Bridges, Dent and Master Tovey

Sir Hubert Parry was the power-broker when Barnby left Eton in 1892. After declining the post of Precentor himself and advising his friend, Walter Parratt, the charismatic Yorkshire-born organist of St George's, Windsor not to accept the job either,[1] he suggested their mutual friend from Oxford days, Charles Harford Lloyd.

'A kindly, gifted and excitable little man who lived in a perpetual state of imagined haste' is how an Eton colleague would later describe the 43-year-old Lloyd. After Oxford, he had travelled as a private tutor to the Vernon-Harcourt family and afterwards to the sons of John Burns of Cunard fame. It was during these tours abroad that he had developed the kind of passion for French and Italian opera which is not vouchsafed to every organ-playing academic. In April 1876, he succeeded S. S. Wesley as organist of Gloucester Cathedral where his pupils included G. R. Sinclair, the future organist of Hereford Cathedral, whose bulldog, Dan, caused him to be immortalised by Elgar in the *Enigma Variations*.[2]

Lloyd's own music is not without distinction. In 1904, Elgar, whom Lloyd had known and encouraged long before wider recognition came Elgar's way, wrote a cadenza for Lloyd's

---

1 That same year, Parratt was appointed Master of the Queen's Musick.
2 Variation 'G.R.S.' A handsome signed photograph of Richard Strauss, which Sinclair had in his possession, was later given to Eton. For many years it hung unnoticed in an obscure corner of the old Music Schools.

F minor Organ Concerto (Gloucester, 1895). His *Service in E flat*, his eight-part *a cappella* 'The righteous shall live for ever more' and his eight-part song 'Thy Rosy Dawn' are among works by Lloyd still occasionally performed. Lloyd was that rare thing, an Organist-Composer-Precentor, so it is perhaps no coincidence that Eton produced a rich crop of composers, academics, and musical administrators during his time as Precentor: Edward J. Dent, Roger Quilter, Lloyd's opera-going and organ-loving friend John Christie, the Australian-born Frederick Kelly, Lord Berners, George Butterworth, Philip Heseltine [Peter Warlock], and Victor Hely-Hutchinson.

That said, Lloyd had the good fortune to be Precentor during that expansive, some would say golden, time which was late-Victorian and Edwardian Eton. A second chapel, for the use of the Lower School, had been dedicated in 1891 and in 1908 a new School Hall was opened. It had (and continues to have) a difficult acoustic but it provided Eton with a sizeable concert venue. The music staff was considerably expanded and it was agreed for the first time that boys could leave morning school for music lessons. A decision was also made, forty years on from the original proposals, to go ahead with the establishing of a Choir School, a small day preparatory school in Brewhouse Yard for sixteen choristers and twelve probationers.

Chapel services continued to be perilous occasions from the disciplinary point of view (on one occasion a boy acquired a supply of explosive tape of the kind used in Christmas crackers and attached it to the inside of hymn books in Lower Chapel) but Lloyd was more than capable of dealing with massed ranks of adolescent boys. Psalm-singing became a particular Eton speciality for the first time since the 1650s, though with a vastly increased output of decibels.

*

Hymn-singing, too, took on a new lease of life – and not just in Eton – thanks, in no small measure, to the pioneering work of a schoolboy survivor from the Eton of the 1850s, Robert Bridges. After Oxford, Bridges had trained and worked as a doctor. When ill health forced his premature retirement from medicine in 1881, he settled with his widowed mother in the village of Yattendon in west Berkshire, married the squire's daughter and flung himself into the somewhat unusual task of reviving and training the church choir. Not surprisingly, the villagers were in awe of him. His friend Edward Marsh was fourteen when he first set eyes on Bridges in Yattendon in 1886:

His noble shaggy head, his big loose-limbed stature, his easy clothes and tropical ties (I remember a bright yellow one, and another which was peacock blue), his grand deep burry voice, and his air of a great gentleman, made the most impressive figure I have known.

Boys as young as five were recruited into the choir which rehearsed assiduously five nights a week. He even saw to it, through the good offices of his father-in-law, that the village school was provided with a musically literate headmaster.

Bridges did, however, have an ulterior motive. Throughout his early years in Yattendon, he was hard at work on *The Yattendon Hymnal*, a pioneering anthology of 100 hymns and hymn tunes which, ever the perfectionist, he published in four exquisitely designed and printed volumes between 1895 and 1899. The Yattendon Hymnal did not pretend to rival *Hymns Ancient and Modern*, the best-selling Victorian anthology which Bridges loathed; but it did have a profound effect on Vaughan Williams's *The English Hymnal* which appeared two years later and which set new standards for what a mass-market publication in this field could achieve.

The opening words of Bridges's preface to *The Yattendon Hymnal* refer to 'the old melodies which it is the chief object of this book to restore to use'. Apart from seven tunes provided by his friend, the painter, musician and critic Harry Ellis Wooldridge, the *Hymnal* contains no music later than the early eighteenth century. Some of the themes and melodies – by composers such as Tallis, Gibbons, Jeremiah Clarke, Purcell, Croft (a Bridges obsession) and Bach – had been central to the Eton choir's repertory two centuries previously and were still extant (in printed form and, occasionally, in performance) during Bridges's time at the school. Was Bridges's taste in such matters – his loathing of Victorian taste-lessness and his sense of an older and better way of doing things – formed during his years at Eton? It is difficult to think otherwise.

Bridges wrote a great deal about hymns and psalmody, most of which is still relevant. Though he took as axiomatic the idea that without dignity a hymn is worthless, he was conscious of the difficulties the church faced. The use of undignified music, he conceded, might be justified in exceptional cases 'which must be left to the judgment of those who consider all things lawful that they may save some'. Another point which he took to be axiomatic was that whereas good music can redeem banal words, fine words cannot redeem banal music. Here, his advice to the clergy was less circumspect:

They must make up their minds on these matters. If they say the hymns which keep me away from church draw others thither, and excite useful religious emotions, then they must take the responsibility wholly on themselves... All I can urge is that they should have at least one service a week where people like myself can attend without being offended or moved to laughter.

*

Of Charles Harford Lloyd's many pupils, no one wielded more power in later life than Edward J. Dent (1876-1957). Elected to a fellowship at King's College, Cambridge in 1902, he taught music in the university until 1918 and returned there as Professor of Music in 1926. Dent revolutionised the teaching of music at Cambridge and did a vast amount for opera. 'Accessibility' (the idea if not the word) was his passion long before the grandparents of Britain's late twentieth-century anti-elitist elite were born. Opera in English was a particular preoccupation, to which end Dent produced more than twenty high-quality singing translations of popular and not-so-popular operas.[3]

Dent was not a clubbable man. Members of the Senior Common Room at King's were always somewhat surprised that E. M. Forster, passionate though he was about music, got on so well with him. As Patrick Wilkinson, Dean and Vice-Provost of King's, later put it, 'there was a certain acidity about [Dent] which one does not associate with Forster'. Whether Forster liked him or not, Dent proved immensely useful to him. The first of his Italian novels, *Where Angels Fear to Tread* owes its title to Dent. (Blackwood's having jibbed at

3 Dent translated a number of Mozart's operas, Beethoven's *Fidelio*, and the great middle-period Verdian trilogy: *Rigoletto, La traviata* and *Il trovatore*. He also translated Flotow's *Martha*, Wagner's *Liebesverbot*, and three operas by Busoni. When Sadler's Wells (now the English National Opera) was founded, Dent's translations were a godsend.

'Monteriano', Dent suggested 'Where Angels Fear to Tread' and, more lamely, 'From a Sense of Duty'.) More importantly, its principal character, Philip Herriton, is largely based on Dent. Forster wrote in a private memorandum:

A useful trick is to look back upon such a person with half-closed eyes, wilfully obscuring certain characteristics. I am then left with about two-thirds of a human being and can get to work. This is what I did with E. J. Dent, who became Philip in *Where Angels*.

Sophisticated, travelled and a brilliant linguist, the opera-loving Dent was largely responsible for Forster's own conversion to opera. In 1901, Forster had told Dent, 'I do not think I shall ever enjoy Italian opera. All the conventions are so irritating'. Eighteen months later, Dent took him to see Donizetti's *Lucia di Lammermoor*, a far from fashionable opera in 1903. (Even in the 1950s, there were those who objected to Maria Callas and Herbert von Karajan 'wasting' their time on the piece.) It must have done the trick. The opera scene in *Where Angels Fear to Tread* (complete with its semi-ironic reference to Flaubert's comparable use of *Lucia di Lammermoor* in *Madame Bovary*) was based on that experience. Forster remembered:

I based this account on a performance I heard at Florence at the beginning of the century where Lucia was sung by a little-known soprano. Her name was Tetrazzini. She had come along in a travelling company from Faenza. We all thought her splendid, but had no conception of her great future and international fame. It is amusing that I should have popped her into my little book without the least idea of her approaching celebrity.

Dent's less attractive side was revealed in 1924 when, under cover of a German-language article on 'Modern English Music' for the *Handbuch der Musikgeschichte*, he launched a furtive attack on Elgar:

Like [Sir Alexander] Mackenzie, he was a violin player by profession, and studied the works of Liszt which were loathsome to conservative academic musicians. He was, moreover, a Catholic, and more or less self-taught, possessing little of the literary culture of Parry or Stanford... For English ears, Elgar's music is too emotional and not wholly free from vulgarity. His orchestral works, Variations, 2 Symphonies, Concertos for Violin and Cello and sundry overtures are lively in colour but pompous in style and with an attempted nobility of expression. His chamber music is... dry and academic.

As a piece of writing it is shoddy, as an example of critical judgment it is arrogant and mean-minded. Philip Heseltine, who had his own doubts about Elgar and who had hitherto enjoyed an amicable relationship with Dent, expressed it rather more circumspectly in a letter he organised in response to an English-language version of the article in 1930. The letter was signed by (among others) Hamilton Harty, John Ireland, Augustus John, George Bernard Shaw, and William Walton. Sent to all the leading British and continental newspapers, it stated:

Professor Dent's failure to appreciate Elgar's music is no doubt temperamental; but it does not justify him in grossly misrepresenting the position which Sir Edward and his music enjoy in the esteem of his fellow-countrymen.

The fact that the attack should have been made when Elgar's reputation was already in serious (albeit temporary) decline should come as no surprise. Dent himself was nothing if not a creature of fashion: an agnostic who could happily write sacred music, a socialist who revelled in the good life. The latter-day emergence of King's as one of Cambridge's trendiest, most Left-leaning and (its famous chapel notwithstanding) most atheistical colleges, owes a lot to the pioneering work of men like Dent.

A rather more attractive character, and a man whose writings live on today in a way which Dent's manifestly do not, was Donald Tovey. Tovey was not educated at Eton but he was born and brought up there. His father, the Revd Duncan Crookes Tovey, a scholar of Trinity College, Cambridge and one of the university chaplains, had moved to Eton in 1874 to teach classics. Donald was born the following year. Duncan Tovey later became Rector of Worplesdon where he combined parish duties with scholarly enquiries into the life and works of Thomas Gray.[4] It is a measure of the affection in which the Toveys – Donald, Duncan and his clever, skittish wife Mary – were held at Eton, by the Warre Cornishes in particular,[5] that on the father's leaving Eton a group of masters presented him with a brand new Broadwood grand for the use of his musically gifted son.

Donald was not only gifted, he was extraordinarily precocious:

There was a sound of clapping in the next room, and Miss Weisse went to the door to look in. A small boy of ten was applauding vigorously,

4 *Gray and his Friends* (Cambridge, 1890/R1985); *The Letters of Thomas Gray* (London 1900-12); *Gray* (London, 1913).

5 Francis Warre Cornish (KS 1853-7, Master 1861-93, Vice-Provost 1893-1916) is one of official Eton's legendary figures but it is his wife, Blanche (1844-1922) who has been more written about. A. C. Benson described her as possessing 'a real touch of genius, a vivid wit, and what was best of all, a rich mine of quite unexpected and even unintentional humour'. In a letter of 26 September, 1917, the young Aldous Huxley reported: 'We spent a strange afternoon in discussing French literature, Hugh Sidgwick and music with that peculiar incoherence that only belongs to conversations with that extraordinary woman; and as we talked we kept rambling into other people's homes and sitting in their drawing rooms and then, as soon as they appeared, going away again.' What Logan Pearsall Smith later called 'the pregnant and startling irrelevancies of Mrs Warre Cornish's conversation' include 'That fugue of Bach's, wasn't it splendid? Wasn't it like becoming a mother?', 'Wagner – what force!', 'Beethoven – how baffling!'.

and the score of a Haydn quartet which he had just finished reading was lying on the table in front of him. He looked up in confusion and said 'Oh, I beg your pardon, I thought I *heard* it'.

Fortunately, Donald was odd in a way which beguiled and refreshed those who came into contact with him. The Warre Cornishes' youngest daughter would recall:

If he had been a conceited boy or a boring one I am sure I should have just run off, bowling my hoop away. Donald's mind was higher altogether than most people's. I felt a sense of something 'going on' when he talked; higher, taller, more distinguished; 'higher up' while I listened below. But when others were there I silently enjoyed the amusing talk he had with my brothers or the grown-ups. I remember a joke he made when a visitor placed a letter for the post out in the hall and asked whether the letter was safe. 'Oh, yes, perfectly safe – it won't go.' Little things like that I still remember, and most amusing jokes at the piano.

One such joke was Tovey's parody of a village choir singing 'God Save the Queen' with gradually descending pitch.

*

Miss Sophie Weisse, the thirty-something lady music-teacher who had overheard Donald applauding Haydn, was the daughter of a concert-pianist. She didn't play herself but had studied with assiduity the teaching methods of the German pedagogue Ludwig Deppe. The 5-year-old Donald had heard from his elder brother that there were singing classes to be had with Miss Weisse at her small private school in Englefield Green on the edge of Windsor Great Park. He went along and remained in her care for the next thirteen years. Duncan Tovey evidently trusted Miss Weisse; when the family moved to Worplesdon, Donald continued to lodge with her during term time.

What most concerned Tovey's father was what he took to be the modest earning-power and low social status of most musicians, the superior lifestyle of the better class of cathedral organist notwithstanding. The event which changed his mind was the appearance in Eton of Miss Weisse's uncle, the great German violinist Joseph Joachim. Donald would recall how Joachim's ambassadorial presence, perfect command of English and profound general culture completely changed his father's view of what a musician could be. 'He never forgot how, when Joachim was told of my progress in Latin and Euclid, he asked, "Does he know it *gründlich* [thoroughly]?"'

Joachim was 49 when he first played in Eton in 1881. He was at the height of his fame. (The Brahms Violin Concerto, dedicated to him, had been unveiled two years earlier.) He offered a magisterial programme which included Bach's D minor Chaconne, Beethoven's *Archduke* Trio and (to the audience's joy and evident relief) arrangements of Brahms's *Three Hungarian Dances*. The *Eton College Chronicle* ventured: 'it is not too much to say that [the recital] will form an epoch in the musical lives of not a few of the audience'.

Tovey's encounters began a few years later. Wary at first, Joachim soon warmed to his niece's talented pupil. He would strum themes from Bach's *Well-Tempered Clavier* on the sitting-room table and ask the boy to identify them. In 1887, he played through the 12-year-old Donald's first Violin Sonata with him. Nor were these merely familial indulgences. On 15 March, 1894, Tovey accompanied Joachim at a public recital in Windsor. The programme began with Brahms's G major Violin Sonata and ended with Beethoven's *Kreutzer* Sonata. Bach's D minor Chaconne (Joachim) and Beethoven's Op. 109 Piano Sonata (Tovey) completed the programme.

★

As a child, Tovey was an inveterate collector of miniature scores. A letter dated 'Christmas Day, 1887' reads:

Dear Miss Weisse,

You're beyond thankability! The scores arrived yesterday safe and sound, and the PASTORAL SYMPHONY arrived today! It's a most bbbbeeeeaaaattttiiiiffffuuuullll Christmas present – it is, it is, it is. When I ordered the Mozart Divertimento for strings and 22 Horns (Oh dear, I didn't mean 22 I meant 2), I expected about eight pages but instead there arrived forty-eight! They're all exceedingly beautiful and I quite admire my choice... I'll also tell you something else. In the list on the back of the Schumann Quintet *all* the Haydns have opus numbers, up to Op.76! I've got five shillings for a Christmas present! Very nice isn't it? I shall soon have to ask them to publish more! At present I want No. 100 (2/-) and No. 3 (6d.) and No. 10 (6d.). Your discount will reduce it to about 2/4d. because last time I got 5/9d. worth for 4/5d.! 1/4d. off.

I am,

Yours affectionately,

Donald F. Tovey

In January 1891 we find him writing:

Dear Miss Weisse,

I got your Postal Order all right, and I thank you for it. I have spent more than a pound, but father has given me 3/6d. I enjoyed my stay at the Alderson's very much, and the *Messiah* was splendid, except Barnbyish and too much left out. I can't help thinking there must be a focus in the Albert Hall; it looks an exact ellipse... I have been to Breitkopf and Härtel's place in Oxford Street, and bought

Mozart – 2 Divertimenti for 2 Flutes, 5 trumpets, 4 drums (!!!)
  "   – Concerto for Flute and Harp!!
  "   – Adagio for Violin and Orchestra (*Loverly*)
  "   – Concerto for Horns!!! (And possibly to play! there are four

of 'em) all as delightful as if for a sane combination of instruments.

Ever your affectionate,

Donald Francis Tovey

★

The remark about Barnby is interesting. By rights, Donald should have studied with him at Eton but Miss Weisse sent him instead to Walter Parratt in Windsor. Later, he studied briefly with Hubert Parry whose methods he evidently relished:

Dr Parry embellishes a pupil's piece of platitudinous ponderosity by extracting the juices of the pupil's brain, and concentrating them into an essence while he mysteriously *increases* the quantity! ... Then we went on waking up a few sleepy places, till we arrove at the development. *Rayther* too long. Spasmodic. Scherzo all right. Dr Parry made me a present of a joke on repetition...

Tovey's six volumes of *Essays in Musical Analysis* (Oxford, 1935-44), which remain to this day classics of their kind, include three essays on Parry. They concern *At a Solemn Music*, *Overture to an Unwritten Tragedy*, and the *Symphonic Variations*, one of Parry's (or anyone else's) most charming works. Tovey's opening paragraph on the Variations offers an amiable tribute to his former teacher:

To the pupils of this great English master these symphonic variations will vividly recall the man. To others the work will assuredly reveal him; not perhaps in such detail as his choral works with their unsurpassable truth and depth in the setting of words; but certainly as pure instrumental music can reveal a character that grounded optimism on a brave recognition of facts, that lost all sense of duty and self-sacrifice in the simple pleasure of goodness, and unconsciously destroyed conceit and priggishness as sunlight destroys germs.

After praising the 'tackling' ('if a Rugby technicality be admissible at Eton') of the snapping woodwind entries in the scherzo section, the essay closes with a tribute to the very ground on which Parry and Tovey were raised:

The violins come rushing in, and soon the work marches to a brilliant close in terms of its own theme – spacious, adequate, and final – with no preaching or tub-thumping to make it seem too small for all that has been devoted to it. Not only the battle of Waterloo was won upon the playing-fields of Eton, but this battle against the Philistines also.

CHAPTER 13

George Butterworth

Like Joah Bates, George Butterworth was an Etonian who hailed from the north country. Like Thomas Arne, he was intended for the law. But there the similarities end. Where Bates was choleric and Arne sleazy, Butterworth was as honest and forthright as the day is long. A colleague who knew him during his brief spell as a schoolmaster at Radley (1909-10) described his 'extraordinary strength of character', his 'rugged directness of manner', his 'intolerance of narrow-mindedness and inefficiency'.

Butterworth died at the age of 31, killed by a sniper's bullet at Pozières during the Battle of the Somme on 5 August 1916, the month in which he was twice recommended for the Military Cross. In a letter of condolence to his father, Sir Alexander Butterworth, General Manager of the North Eastern Railway Company in York, Ralph Vaughan Williams wrote: 'I think I know of no composer whose music expressed his character more exactly... He had the determination to be and say exactly what he meant'.

Butterworth arrived in Eton as a King's Scholar in 1899. He studied with Charles Lloyd and his talented assistant Thomas Dunhill (1877-1946) and was further helped by the fact that Goodhart was his housemaster. One of the earliest occasions on which Butterworth's name appears (part of a quartet of pianists in a *Marche militaire* by Schubert) is at a birthday concert given in Goodhart's honour in June 1901. Thereafter,

Butterworth's name crops up regularly in concert notices in the *Eton College Chronicle*, culminating in the concert on 2 April, 1903 when he conducted his *Barcarolle* for orchestra.[1] In 1910 he returned to the school to take part in a concert of works composed and performed by Old Etonians, the first of its kind. The concert included part of Parry's *Introduction and Fugue* played by Butterworth, the first performance (in piano duo form) of Butterworth's own *Rhapsody on English Folk Tunes*, and three of Quilter's Shakespeare song settings sung by Christopher Stone accompanied by Quilter himself.

Research into folk-song and folk-dance was Butterworth's principal passion. Time spent at the Royal College of Music, Radley, and *The Times* newspaper was little more than a backdrop to the researches he pursued in the company of leading practitioners of the day: Cecil Sharp, Vaughan Williams, and Old Etonian Francis Jekyll. It was not a fashionable activity. Associating with the peasantry was seen as being anti-establishment. It is said that when Sir Hugh Allen spied Butterworth and R. O. Morris approaching Blackwell's in The Broad in Oxford, he rumbled: 'There goes more red revolution than in the whole of Russia'. Butterworth brooked no nonsense from such people. He once took a group of folk-dancers to tea at the Savoy Hotel in London where, with a mixture of north country grit and Etonian *savoir faire*, he resisted all attempts by the management to have them removed to a more suitable eating-place.

His happiest days were spent tramping the Sussex Downs with Jekyll and Vaughan Williams in search of extinct or near-

1 Subsequently lost or destroyed. The *Eton College Chronicle* noted that 'Butterworth's appearance was the signal for a torrent of applause' but was silent on the subject of the music itself.

extinct songs and dances. He studied Morris Dancing in the West Midlands and travelled with Cecil Sharp to the northeast of England to study the dying art of sword-dancing. He was a superb researcher, meticulous and sharp-witted with what one colleague called 'a genius for avoiding a false scent'. He was also a superb dancer, a skill he transferred to his compositions. 'Music rots when it gets too far from the dance', the poet Ezra Pound wisely observed. The first of Butterworth's *Two English Idylls* is a fine illustration of the potency of dance, in particular the oboe's enunciation of the Sussex folk-song 'Dabbling the dew' with which the first *Idyll* begins.

The handful of Butterworth's compositions which have come down to us (he destroyed a good deal before leaving for France in 1914) reveal a distinctive voice somewhat towards the *avant garde* end of the English Edwardian style. *The Banks of Green Willow*, rich in play and melancholy, has many fine original details. Even more compelling is his orchestral rhapsody *A Shropshire Lad*, based on Butterworth's own setting of Housman's 'Loveliest of trees'. The eloquence of the orchestral writing and the anger felt at the work's climax have an almost Wagnerian reach. Few orchestral tone-poems of the period are more finely shaped and imagined.[2]

Housman's *A Shropshire Lad* (1896) turns out in retrospect to have been one of the defining works of the period up to and including the First World War. Pseudo folk-ballads set in a mythical Shropshire landscape, they chronicle death,

2 The great Hungarian conductor Arthur Nikisch conducted the première with the London Symphony Orchestra at the Leeds Festival on 2 October, 1913. He took suggestions from Butterworth at the first run-through, did not rehearse them, recalled every detail from memory at the final rehearsal, and conducted a near-perfect performance.

mutability and loss in an increasingly agnostic world. Housman was thinking in particular of the young lads killed in the colonial wars *c*.1880, the very men in whose memory Eton had erected its new organ screen in 1882. In practice, the poems took on newer and more terrible resonances during the First World War, much as Gustav Mahler's songs *Revelge* (1899) and *Der Tamboursg'sell* (1901) would do. *A Shropshire Lad* mourns, too, the vanishing of pastoral vision and, by devolution, the death of the old imagined England.

Butterworth completed his settings of six songs from *A Shropshire Lad* in 1911 and gave the manuscripts (all except 'On the idle hill of summer') to Eton in April 1912. They are dedicated to Victor Annesley Barrington-Kennett (Eton 1901-5, Oxford 1906-10, killed at Serre on 13 March, 1916). This justly celebrated cycle has rather eclipsed Butterworth's other song-settings: for instance, the eleven Sussex folk-songs, one of which, Henley's 'Love Blows as the Wind Blows', Butterworth later orchestrated.

The moment Butterworth joined up in 1914, music was set aside. The last glimpse we have of Butterworth the musician is in July 1914. Vaughan Williams had taken the score of *Hugh the Drover* to Oxford where it was seen by Butterworth, Hugh Allen, and Henry Ley, a future Eton Precentor. At midnight, the party decided to walk to Boar's Hill. Ley remembers Butterworth standing on Allen's doorstep in Keble Road shouting 'Madmen!'. It was no haphazard insult. As dawn approached, Vaughan Williams, attempting an improvised short-cut, found himself stranded on top of a chicken shed.

*

In Leeds in 1910, Butterworth had attended the première of Vaughan Williams's *Sea Symphony* in the company of Henry Ley and others. Deeply impressed, he urged Vaughan Williams to write a purely orchestral symphony. Vaughan Williams would recall:

He had been sitting with us one evening, smoking and playing (I like to think it was one of those rare occasions when we persuaded him to play his beautiful little pianoforte piece, *Firle Beacon*) and at the end of the evening, as he was getting up to go, he said in his characteristically abrupt way: 'You know, you ought to write a symphony'. From that moment the idea of a symphony – a thing which I had always declared I would never attempt – dominated my mind. I showed the sketches to George bit by bit as they were finished, and it was then that I realised that he possessed, in common with very few composers, a wonderful power of criticism of other men's work, and insight into their ideas and motives.

A London Symphony, as Vaughan Williams called it, had its first performance under the direction of Geoffrey Toye in London's Queen's Hall on 27 March, 1914. When no English publisher could be found for the symphony, Vaughan Williams sent it, on Tovey's advice, to Breitkopf und Härtel in Leipzig. This invited a second intervention by Butterworth. Concerned about the imminence of war with Germany, he suggested that a copy be made from the band parts which were still in London. This he duly did, helped by Butterworth, Dent and Toye. After the war, Vaughan Williams revised the symphony on no fewer than three occasions.[3] Butterworth was named as its posthumous dedicatee.

3 The original 1913 version was recorded for the first time in December 2000 by Richard Hickox and the London Symphony Orchestra. Public performance of the unrevised score remains prohibited.

As Vaughan Williams asked at the time of Butterworth's death, 'What might have been? We can never know, but we can cherish what remains to us.' Vaughan Williams served in the Ambulance Corps. His own war requiem is his Third Symphony, *Pastoral*. But it is the *London* Symphony which stands for the lost generation which died in the war, with Butterworth as its representative figure. At the end of the score, Vaughan Williams quotes from H. G. Wells's novel *Tono-Bungay*:

Light after light goes down. England and the Kingdom, Britain and the Empire, the old prides and the old devotions, glide abeam, astern, sink down under the horizon, pass – pass. The river passes, London passes, England passes.

It has been said that Britain lost both world wars: the first, genetically, the second, economically. There is no more eloquent confirmation of the genetic catastrophe than the names on the war memorials which line the cloisters at Eton. These names tell their own tale but the bare statistics are compelling enough. 5,687 Etonians served in the war. 1,160 were killed and 1,467 were wounded. There were 13 VCs, 548 DSOs, and 744 MCs, many of them, like Butterworth's, awarded posthumously.

CHAPTER 14

Lord Berners

Thirty-one of the First World War British generals, the so-called 'asses leading donkeys', were Etonians. In 1916, the honorary British *attaché* in Rome, Lord Berners, wrote his *Trois petits marches funèbres*, the first of which is entitled 'Pour un homme d'état' ('For a Statesman'). It begins with a strangely disjunct reference to the opening of Beethoven's Fifth Symphony: an epic raspberry aimed at the generals and politicians, safe in their oak-panelled rooms, who were sending the flower of European youth to the charnel-house.

Like a number of Etonians of his generation, Berners adored Wagner whilst at the same time reserving the right to mock the occasionally ludicrous solemnity of German Romantic art. During the war, he wrote his *Three Songs in the German Manner*. Part parody, part tribute, the sequence begins with 'Du bist wie eine Blume' in which the subject of adoration is not a girl but a prize white pig. Coming as it does complete with grunts in the left-hand piano part, it is a song Lord Emsworth might have been pleased to hear in the drawing-room at Blandings Castle. The second song is a Hugo Wolf parody, the third, 'Weihnachtslieder', mocks the German preoccupation with Christmas. It is the sign of a master that the piano-writing is memorable in its own right; no wonder Stravinsky admired the cycle.

*

Gerald Tyrwhitt-Wilson arrived at Eton, aged thirteen and a half, in the spring of 1897. He was already fond of music, despite the fact that his mother – described by Harold Nicolson as having the face of Mr Gladstone and the brain of a peahen – was deeply suspicious of intellectual activity in general and musical activity in particular. (When Gerald mentioned that Richard Strauss had based a new opera on Wilde's *Salomé*, his mother simply murmured 'Oh, hush, dear'.)

In his *A Distant Prospect*, Berners claims that Eton at the turn of the century was a place richly peopled with sons of the aristocracy, country gentlemen, and the higher echelons of the military where games took precedence over scholarship and where 'character' took precedence over intellect. The first master he was up to was Mr 'Hoppy' Daman. Berners remarks: 'A stranger visiting his division-room might well have imagined that knock-about humour was one of the subjects taught at Eton'. The only 'great' teacher he admits to encountering at Eton was Arthur Benson.

The dining-room in his boarding house was equipped with a piano on which he attempted to play some of the Chopin *Nocturnes*:

Although the piano had acquired through age a harpsichord-like quality more suitable to Scarlatti than Chopin, the mere touch of the keys after so long an abstinence was a joy to me. I had not been playing long when the door was opened and a boy called Ainslie appeared. He was a most important person, a member of Library, that Council of Ten that stood in the same relation to individual houses as 'Pop' did to the school in general. I jumped up from the music-stool in panic.

Ainslie returned with a entourage of fellow grandees and asked Gerald to repeat what he had just played. Less well disposed observers of Gerald's new-found favour with members of the Library concluded that he had become their catamite. Though he was a good-looking teenager – he would describe himself in later life as 'short, swarthy, bald, dumpy, and simian' – this does not appear to have been the case.

Finding other music-loving boys in the school was not impossible. The results, however, were rarely satisfactory. One boy, Wilson, was a good pianist but, like many precociously talented musicians, he seemed more interested in what he could do with the music than in the music itself. By contrast, Wilson's friend, Delmer, was a fogeyish academic type who dismissed Gerald's beloved Chopin with a wave of the hand: 'The man could never have written a good fugue.'

Gerald was advised to take up rowing to bolster his image. This resulted in palpitations and further ignominy when he came last:

> However, the blackest hour comes before the dawn, and at this point there entered into my life two new factors to raise once more my flagging spirits; one of them was Wagner; the other a boy called Deniston.

Deniston, a beguiling Machiaval, was, to put no finer point on it, the school tart [1]. To philistine opinion, however, Wagner was a greater threat to Gerald's moral well-being than Deniston. All Gerald could initially afford in the Wagner line was *A Synopsis of Wagner's Nibelungen Ring* which he bought from a local bookshop. Then he saw in the window of a music-shop in Windsor the vocal score of *Das Rheingold*. In his autobiography, he says that his father, making an unexpected visit to Windsor, gave him the money for the score:

> I turned the passages feverishly. There they were, the Rhinemaidens

---

1 A family trait. Deniston's mother, Kitty, was 'a friend' of the Prince of Wales.

swimming about in semi-quavers, Alberich climbing up from the depths of the Rhine to the accompaniment of syncopated quavers and rising arpeggios, the theft of gold followed by a scurry of descending scales out of which emerged the majestic strains of the Valhall motif.

At home, Gerald built his own miniature Wagner theatre out of a derelict dolls' house which had belonged to his mother. Meanwhile, at Eton he had become friendly with a small, bespectacled, rather ugly and extremely odd boy by the name of Bartlett. Bartlett enquired of Gerald whether he was interested in pantomime. Gerald had a dim recollection of there being a 'Pantomime' in Debussy's *L'Enfant prodigue*. Bartlett replied that it was not at all like that and proceeded to lure Gerald into playing the piano while he acted out, in a series of bizarre gyrations, such light-hearted subjects as 'The Soul of Man in Conflict with the Universe' and 'Ideal Beauty emerging from the Chrysalis of Materialism'. Deniston was not impressed.

Berners left Eton bereft of book-learning but a good deal wiser as to some of the stranger pastimes of his fellow men. As a composer, he was largely self-taught, though he did take a number of lessons in counterpoint with Donald Tovey. This gave rise to the joke, 'Berners studied music in England with one of the more orthodox professors, as a result of which he entered the diplomatic service'. In fact, he made no mark whatsoever as a diplomat and a very considerable mark as a musician. Sir Thomas Armstrong, whom Berners sought out when Armstrong was an organ scholar at Keble College, Oxford, would later say of him:

His was the most alert and far-seeing brain that I ever had to do with music. You only had to mention one of the rules that guided Palestrina and Berners at once knew why the rule had arisen and what was its musical purpose.[2]

Like fellow Etonian, Philip Heseltine, Berners knew a vast amount about Elizabethan music and literature. The first of his *Three English Songs* (1920) is an exquisite setting of a song from an early Jacobean drama by Thomas Dekker, *Patient Grissel*. Yet it is an earnest of his breadth of sympathies that the same cycle also includes a setting of an extremely angry contemporary poem by Robert Graves, 'The Lady in the Pauper Ward', in which a frustrated relative is heard to cry, 'Why do you churn smooth water rough again / Selfish old skin and bone?'.

This was not entirely typical. Like Rossini, Berners was more than happy to cultivate for the world at large a mask of casual unconcern. He was certainly happy to be thought odd: dyeing the pigeons at his home in Berkshire or placing a clavichord in the back of his Rolls-Royce the better to frighten French peasants as he swept through their Provençal villages strumming the keyboard and leering at passers-by through a devil-mask. He knew from his days at Eton that in England it does no harm to be thought slightly mad if one intends to be serious about art. In his novel *Far from the Madding War* (1941) he presents himself in the guise of the eccentric Lord FitzCricket:

He was always referred to by the gossip-column writers as 'the versatile peer', and indeed there was hardly a branch of art in which he had not at one time or other dabbled. He composed music, he wrote books, he

2 When Oxford University Press commissioned a dozen English composers to provide transcriptions of Bach, Berners chose the Christmastide organ prelude 'In dulci jubilo'.

painted; he did a great many things with a certain facile talent. He was astute enough to realise that, in Anglo-Saxon countries, art is more highly appreciated if accompanied by a certain measure of eccentric publicity. This fitted in well with his natural inclinations.

Anyone interested in promoting a stereotypical image of Berners as the aristocratic devil-may-care Old Etonian can point to 'Come On, Algernon', the famously saucy music-hall song about Daisy 'the girl who asked for more' he wrote for the 1944 film *Champagne Charlie*, or the exquisite 'Red Roses and Red Noses' which he provided for Edith Sitwell's children's anthology *Look, the Sun!* in 1941. They will also cite the numerous off-the-cuff put-downs and witticisms. The man who described T. E. Lawrence as 'always backing into the limelight' and who scrawled on the title page of Cyril Connolly's *Enemies of Promise* 'Or Why Can't I Write a Book?' is the same man who declined Siegfried Sassoon's offer of a ticket to hear Beethoven's Ninth Symphony with the simple admonition, 'Nothing will induce me to go and hear the Ninth Symphony'.

It was this aspect of Berners, along with his fastidiousness and high intelligence, which drew him to composers such as Rossini and Satie.[3] Did he know Rossini's late piano piece 'Un petit train de plaisir' which involves a train crash, the flight of the victims' souls to heaven, and the sardonic coda in which the heirs of the more well-to-do victims cut celebratory capers? Berners's own 'Pour une tante à héritage' is rather less cruel. It does, however, carry the mischievous subtitle 'Enfin, nous allons pouvoir acheter une automobile'.

---

3 Like Eric Satie (and, later, Tom Lehrer), Berners favoured droll score annotations such as 'Slow down politely' or 'Very seriously silent'.

Musically, the satire could be devastating. As Constant Lambert observed after hearing Berners's brief three-movement *Fantaisie espagnole*, it is more or less impossible ever again to listen to Falla or Ravel in 'Spanish' mood with a straight face. Berners loved popular songs and rollicking sea-shanties but he was impatient of the Cecil Sharp – Butterworth – Vaughan Williams folk-song movement which he mocks unmercifully in his incomparable 'Dialogue between Tom Filuter and his man by Ned the Dog Stealer'.

'An amateur who wasn't at all amateurish' was Stravinsky's view of this beguilingly amusing English Milord. He described bars 41-4 of Berners's 'Valse brillante' (from *Valses bourgeoises*, 1919) as 'one of the most impudent passages in modern music'. It will come as no surprise to anyone who knows the real Lord Berners that he was for a time also seriously interested in the music of Schoenberg; though he would later conclude that atonalism 'has proved infertile, an enclosed, dry, rocky academic valley with no issue'. When Compton Mackenzie invited various personalities in the musical world to nominate their favourite songs, singers, and composers for the 1926 Christmas issue of *The Gramophone*, Berners replied:

My favourite song is 'The Last Rose of Summer'; my favourite composer, Bach; my favourite tune is the third of Schönberg's six pieces for pianoforte, because it is so obscure that no one is ever likely to grow tired of it (which you must admit is as good a reason for preferring a tune as any other); and if by 'singer' you mean any kind of singer then the one I prefer is Little Tich. But, on the other hand, if you mean merely concert singers, please substitute Clara Butt.

Roy Plomley never got round to inviting Berners onto *Desert Island Discs*, the programme he had devised for the BBC in 1942. Nothing daunted, Berners made his own selection:

Kurt Weill excerpts from *Mahagonny*
Bach Concerto for 3 Pianos in C, 3rd movement
Liszt Hungarian Rhapsody No. 2
    Viennese Seven Singing Sisters (Regal Zonophone MR 1755)
Tchaikovsky Symphony No. 4, 3rd movement (pizzicato)
Berners *Triumph of Neptune*, 'Polka'
Chabrier *Marche Joyeuse*
Stravinsky *Jeu de cartes*
Ravel Piano Concerto [which one is not specified] last movement

'Charming or stimulating music that appeals to the senses rather than the intellect' was his criterion. The Bach, he conceded, appeals to the intellect 'but it is so stimulating that I feel it ought to exhilarate even the most lowbrow of listeners'. To those who thought his choice 'capricious, over-catholic and impure', he confessed a dislike of certain composers – Wagner, Brahms, Sibelius, Delius – whose music had been the subject of a 'too enthusiastic adulation in certain quarters'. His own enthusiasms, in chronological order of their discovery, were: Chopin, Wagner, Richard Strauss, Debussy, Schoenberg, and Stravinsky. The Nazis' exploitation of Wagner had rather dulled that particular enthusiasm but Berners continued to enjoy the music of Richard Strauss, in particular *Till Eulenspiegel* and the incidental music for *Le bourgeois gentilhomme*. And as he began to tire of Schoenberg, so he had turned more and more to Stravinsky, Bartók and the young Benjamin Britten.

Berners chose just one of his own pieces, the polka from *The Triumph of Neptune*, a Diaghilev commission, chore-ographed by Balanchine in 1926. The recording, Berners added, should be the one conducted by Sir Thomas Beecham.

Appropriately so. Beecham was that other great British musical amateur who 'wasn't at all amateurish'.

Jerusalem

The idea for a national hymn based on the opening verses of William Blake's *Milton* came from Robert Bridges in the early months of 1916. A lobby group calling itself 'Fight for Right' had been formed with the aim of providing counterblasts to a new German propaganda offensive on the 'justice' of the war.

The lobby was the brainchild of Sir Francis Younghusband (1863-1942), a not entirely savoury character described in the *Dictionary of National Biography* as 'soldier, diplomat, geographer, and mystic'. (He was also a mountaineer, a moving spirit behind the earliest attempts to climb Mount Everest.) Bridges determined to approach Hubert Parry and, if he refused the commission, George Butterworth. Parry had his doubts about Younghusband but it was a strong idea which quickly took on a life of its own. The composer Walford Davies would recall in a letter to *The Times* published in 1927:

Sir Hubert Parry gave me the manuscript of this setting of Blake's 'Jerusalem' one memorable morning in 1916... We looked at it long together in his room at the Royal College of Music, and I recall vividly his unwonted happiness over it. One momentary act of his should perhaps be told here. He ceased to speak, and put his finger on the note D in the second stanza where the words 'O clouds unfold' break his rhythm. I do not think any word passed about it, yet he made it perfectly clear that this was the one note and one moment of the song which he treasured... I copyrighted it in the composer's name and published it in 1916. We needed it for the men at the time.

The stirring melody, subtle phraseology and – in Elgar's re-orchestration of 1922 – sonic grandeur of the piece ensured its place among a select group of unofficial English national anthems.

In more recent times there have been those who would dearly like to have both *Jerusalem* and *Land of Hope and Glory* outlawed from the Last Night of the Proms. Parry himself was no jingoist. 'Fight for Right' pressed him to write more in the same vein (James Frazer of *Golden Bough* fame was the new intermediary) but Parry refused. In May 1917, he wrote to Younghusband withdrawing his support from 'Fight for Right' altogether.

Jerusalem continued to be sung by the jingoists but it was a performance by the Women's Movement on 17 March, 1917, conducted by Parry himself, which opened up very different possibilities for the piece. In March 1918, he gave permission for it to be used as the official hymn of the suffragette movement. He wrote to the leader of the movement, the 71-year-old Mrs Henry Fawcett:

I wish indeed it might become the Women Voters Hymn, as you suggest. People seem to enjoy singing it. And having the vote ought to diffuse a good deal of joy too. So they would combine happily.

Nowadays *Jerusalem* is the official hymn of the Women's Institutes, a generally less militant movement than 'Fight for Right' or the suffragettes.

CHAPTER 15

Voluptuaries of the imagination

Harold Acton, Edward Sackville-West, Cyril Connolly

Armistice Day 1918 was declared a whole holiday at Eton. The entire school marched down the High Street waving flags and cheering till throats were hoarse. Later that day Harold Acton found himself in St George's Chapel, an experience he would later recall in prose of the deepest purple in *Memoirs of an Aesthete*:

> The notes of the organ swelled upwards and flew like invisible wings: long pent-up spirits of joy were suddenly released and shook the dusty banners above our heads. The mellow chapel trembled as if Samson were in our midst and his muscles were straining to the utmost in a paean of victory. Surely the roof would come tottering down… yet one was not afraid. This was victory! And instead of falling the roof had been raised by those spirits of joy. It had floated into the empyrean. Great Heaven was above us, serene, and we could see the highest stars as never before. The flags and the bunting withered after that vision. Only organs can celebrate victory as it should be celebrated.

The war over, hedonism took hold and, for what was possibly the first time in the school's history, the aesthetes set the tone. Acton described himself and his closest friends at Eton – Alan Clutton-Brock, Robert Byron, Henry Green, Oliver Messel, Anthony Powell, and Cyril Connolly ('who puffed cynically on our fringe') – as 'voluptuaries of the imagination'. As Connolly himself puts it in *Enemies of Promise*: 'Eton was our Eden and gave us grace, greenness and security, the security to rebel, the greenness to worship and the grace to love'.

Music was all around them. Acton was enrolled in the Musical Society (despite deliberately sabotaging his voice test) where he rebelled by singing the original Italian words to the glorious Neapolitan song 'Santa Lucia' while his fellow Etonians bawled out a somewhat blunter English version. Mozart and Marvell were Acton's twin gods, urbane, gracious and tinged with melancholy. There was no Mozart in that first Musical Society concert, but there was at least one piece to gladden the apprentice aesthete's heart:

To me the most significant number was a solo performance by Edward Sackville-West. He was older than I but appeared minute at the grand piano, where he proceeded to pound through *L'Isle joyeuse*. To hear Debussy at all was to banish the spiritual loneliness that had oppressed me since I left Italy. It was like a promise of intellectual freedom, and I left the concert in a mood of rare elation.

*

The degree to which music, officially and unofficially, now permeated Eton, more so than at most comparable schools of the time, was one of the reasons why Edward Sackville-West had been sent there. He was in Manor House whose house-master, Samuel Lubbock, had survived a determined challenge from Goodhart for the hand in marriage of Irene Scharrer, a cousin of Myra Hess, and a gifted pianist in her own right.[1] Though Eton now had several first-rate piano teachers on its staff, Miss Scharrer acquired her own circle of precociously gifted boys: Edward Sackville-West, Lord Morven Cavendish Bentinck, Alan Pryce-Jones and others. She occasionally played at concerts. On 18 December, 1916 she

1 Conductors of the eminence of Richter and Nikisch engaged her. Elgar spoke of her in connection with his (uncompleted) Piano Concerto.

and Eddy played *A Waltz Pageant* by Frederick Kelly, the Australian-born, Eton-educated composer, virtuoso pianist, oarsman, hell-raiser, and all-round good fellow who had been killed in action at Beaucourt-sur-Ancre the previous month.[2]

Sackville-West was abnormally fragile. At the time of his death in 1965, an obituary notice by *The Times* Music Critic William Mann noted: 'Frail, pale and slight like a portrait by El Greco, he was possessed of a nervous temperament which showed itself in uncompromising fastidiousness and in occasional fits of intense melancholy.' Frances Partridge has left an extraordinary sketch of Sackville-West listening to music (a piece by Liszt) towards the end of his life. He was, she recalls in her diary:

like a cat that has swallowed a saucer of cream, his face bristling with carefully controlled sensual relish according amusingly with its neat oval; foot and head waving and his unexpectedly square strong hands from time to time accompanying the pianist with a rapid trill on the arm of his chair. His excitement over this to him entirely congenial music caused him to make quick darting rushes about the room like a water-beetle to look at the score, or – once – play a few bars on the neglected piano.

Had he not been so nervous and so frail – and cursed, too, with an incurable susceptibility to nose-bleeds – it is possible that Sackville-West might have become a professional pianist.

2 F. S. Kelly (1881-1916). Most worthy of revival are a number of Kelly's songs and the *Elegy* for strings and harps (1915) written in memory of his close friend Rupert Brooke, with whom he served at Gallipoli and whom he would help lay to rest on the Greek island of Skyros. Kelly's diary entry of the event would have pleased the scholar-pagans back in Eton: 'The small olive grove in the narrow valley and the scent of the wild sage gave a strong classical tone which was so in harmony with the poet we were burying that to some of us the Christian ceremony seemed out of keeping.'

In the event, he hovered productively on the periphery of national musical life. In 1925, he published *Piano Quintet*, a rare example of a novel which engages, celebrates and understands music and musicians. Later, he fell in love with the young Benjamin Britten ('My dear White Child' as he calls him in his letters). The affair was never consummated, Britten was already spoken for, but Sackville-West advised on the choice of poems for the *Serenade for Tenor, Horn and Strings*, which is dedicated to him, and Britten would provide the incidental music for Sackville-West's 1943 BBC commission *The Rescue*, 'A Melodrama for Broadcasting based on Homer's Odyssey'.

The Rescue is a period piece but *Piano Quintet* merits republication. Those critics who in 1999 welcomed Vikram Seth's *An Equal Music* with such phrases as 'the finest novel about music ever written in English' had presumably never heard of *Piano Quintet* with which *An Equal Music* shares certain similarities. In Sackville-West's novel, a European journey by five musicians to Paris, Dijon, Berlin, Triebelstadt and Vienna is the background to what becomes a fraught three-way game of emotional hide-and-seek between Imogen, Aurelian and the pianist Melchior who has joined the quartet for the César Franck Quintet. The story builds towards its climax first at a concert in Triebelstadt where Melchior watches as the quartet plays Brahms, Schubert and Beethoven (the sublime A minor Quartet, Op. 132), then in Vienna where, during a performance of *Der Rosenkavalier* at the State Opera conducted by Strauss himself, Imogen recognises herself in the figure of the Marschallin 'this quiet symbol of self-defeated love'.

Piano Quintet was Sackville-West's first novel. Not surprisingly, perhaps, it grows in assurance as it proceeds. (The end is worthy of the young Henry James.) Seth's may be the more practised work of fiction but Sackville-West has an unrivalled touch where the music itself is concerned, both in the set pieces (the *Der Rosenkavalier* chapter is a minor *tour de force*) and in the fleeting asides:

He played a *Sonatina* of Busoni – a brief icy interlude of the purest intellectual ecstasy. Major and minor keys questioned and answered one another, throwing a shuttle of harmony through a world of two listeners. There was no sense of restlessness in the tiny work: it wove its own peace in the completion of itself. It rounded its own circle calmly, without a throb of burning emotion. And it ended as quietly and starkly as it had begun.[3]

In 1945 Sackville-West, his friend Eardley Knollys and the music critic Desmond Shawe-Taylor acquired a Queen Anne rectory at Long Crichel near Wimborne in Dorset. It was there that he and Shawe-Taylor worked on *The Record Guide*, a series of authoritative, elegantly written, finely produced volumes on the available recordings of the day. The entries are unsigned but it takes no great forensic skill to determine authorship. Who but Sackville-West himself could have said of Toscanini's recording of Beethoven's Ninth Symphony:

At the climax of the first movement, where the main theme returns in the major key, the listener has the strange sensation of being at the heart of the whirlwind: he feels impelled to leave his chair and pace the room.

Or this, midway through an unforgettable short essay on Chopin:

The aristocratic·young dandy with the dreamy eyes, the innocent mouth, the high nose and the long fair hair no doubt existed; it is the

3 *Sonatina* No. 4, 'In diem nativitas Christi MCMVII'

Chopin of the Rubio portrait and of the Nocturne in E flat. But Chopin was not always like that: if we turn to the daguerreotype made in the year of his death, we receive a shock. The eyes look morose and there are pouches under them; the mouth has widened and coarsened with pain; the whole face is deeply lined with illness and embitterment. He looks angry at having been interrupted for a moment in his work. This is the Chopin of the last Nocturnes and Mazurkas, of the Sonatas, the Fantaisie and the F minor Ballade.[4]

Sackville-West left Eton in 1919. It was a wrench personally but something of a relief musically. He described his last recital, in which he played works by Chopin and Debussy, as truly awful:

The audience apathetic and somnolent, consisting entirely of dames and tutors' wives. The head beak wisely sat in his study & read all the time. I played the Étude *atrociously*, but the rest quite fairly well. But *quel atmosphère*!

*

There was a quite different *atmosphère* developing elsewhere in Eton. Dyson's, the jewellers and watchmakers in Eton High Street, provided an upstairs back room where it was possible to hire a gramophone and play one's own records. Acton, Brian Howard, and Henry Yorke (the novelist-to-be Henry Green) regularly hired the room where they affected to perform a number of the great Nijinsky roles to the accompaniment of the gramophone. As Acton would recall: 'Without having seen Massine's performance of the Miller's dance in *The Three-cornered Hat*, Brian would stamp his heels and snap his fingers at de Falla's rhythms and produce a creditable

4 *The Record Guide* (London, 1951), p. 162; Revised Edition (London, 1955), p. 188. The books are long out of print but second-hand copies are not difficult to come by.

equivalent'. Many musicians scorned the gramophone; Acton, a passionate amateur, adored it: 'Often a record from *Petrushka* or *Sylphides* would warm one like a sun bath on a bleak November day and supply new the vitamins which were lacking in our other food'.

In the light of these highly unconventional cavortings (Hornby must have been spinning in his grave) is there any wonder that Aldous Huxley, an Etonian who had briefly returned to teach at his old school, should have written in 1947, 'I have never been able to agree with the current platitude about our public schools standardising and suppressing originality'?

★

Eton's Head Master between 1917 and 1933 was Dr Cyril Alington, who was something of an original in his own right. An Old Marlburian, he had been Goodhart's successor as Master-in-College before going on to become Head Master of Shrewsbury. With their shared passion for Gilbert and Sullivan, Goodhart and Alington were soon back in harness again. When A. P. Herbert wrote a tongue-in-cheek piece in *Punch* suggesting that the study of the Classics was bad for Eton boys' morals, Alington dashed off a response which Goodhart promptly set to music as a G & S patter song. The first stanza reads:

> Sir, what is the use
> Of pretending that Zeus
> Sets the tone of behaviour at Eton?
> Any boy who began
> To behave like a swan
> Would be promptly and properly beaten.

144

Alington and Goodhart later wrote their own full-length G&S operetta, *King Harrison*. The work was published though (in as much as it is possible to ascertain such things) never performed professionally.

★

Acton's remark about Cyril Connolly 'puffing cynically at our fringe' was less than just. Connolly was not a cynic. He was, rather, a dandified yet highly intelligent Colleger who noticed some of the cracks in the aesthetes' (and Eton's) facade. His first impressions of Eton had been predictably agreeable. On a visit from his prep school one warm summer's afternoon, he found himself on Windsor Bridge:

> ... everything seemed splendid and decadent, the huge stale elms, the boys in their many-coloured caps and blazers, the top hats, the strawberries and cream, the smell of wisteria. I looked over the bridge as a boy in an outrigger came gliding past, like a waterboatman. Two Etonians were standing on the bridge and I heard one remark, 'Really that man Wilkinson's not at all a bad oar'. The foppish drawl, the two boys with their hats on the back of their heads, the graceful sculler underneath, seemed the incarnation of elegance and maturity.

It was a first glimpse of what Connolly would call 'the civilisation of the lilies', rooted in the past, effete, decadent. When he reached Eton as a King's Scholar, he found that, even in College, the English distrust of intellect, and a prejudice in favour of the amateur, persisted: 'To be "highbrow" was to be different, to be set apart and so excluded from the ruling class of which one was either a potential enemy or a potential servant'.

What had survived at Eton was the tradition of classical

humanism as laid down in the eighteenth century and perpetuated by Johnson, Browning, Luxmoore, Howard Sturgis, Austen Leigh, and the Provost, M. R. James. In *Enemies of Promise*, Connolly characterises Eton classics as being too much in love with the purple patch: Homer was somewhat Wagnerised, Virgil filled with a *fin-de-siècle* morbid distress. It was all vaguely but deliciously decadent: 'For the culture of the lilies, rooted in the past, divorced from reality, and dependent on a dead foreign tongue, was by nature sterile'. Eton's true originals – Huxley and Keynes, Orwell (and he might have added Berners, Butterworth, and Heseltine) – 'did not wear like Maurice Baring, Arthur Benson, Percy Lubbock or J. K. Stephen, a halo of the pale-blue canon'.

Connolly loved music in his own self-regarding and somewhat world-weary way. He had no interest whatsoever in the lives of composers or anything so vulgar as technicalities. His letters to Noel Blakiston are full of solipsistic reveries. Ravel's *Mother Goose*, he writes, 'seemed to express all my mood complex, better even than [Wagner's] *Forest Murmurs*; with its picture of the rainy leafy troubled woods and the tragedy known only to a few birds'. Of Debussy's String Quartet, he observed: 'I play it on wet days but it is not summer music'. The Ravel Quartet is 'that dayspring of anguish'. Dvorak's *New World Symphony*, which he buys by mistake, turns out to be 'very satisfying, strangely so for a popular and vaguely barbarous piece'.

In his final year, Connolly was unexpectedly elected to that most prestigious of Eton institutions, Eton Society or 'Pop' as it is more familiarly known, an election which caused him to modify his lifestyle. Ashamed, now, to be seen hiring classical records from Dyson's, he would go there to play 'Say it with

Music', 'while the fox-trot floated away on the sunlight and we commented on the looks of the passers by'.

He did, however, hold a spectacular leaving tea 'to which my friends were invited in platonic couples and where I played the *Après-midi d'un faune* on my gramophone'.

CHAPTER 16

Warlockry

On the opening page of Aldous Huxley's novel *Antic Hay* (1923), Theodore Gumbril, B.A. (Oxon) sits in his oaken stall, in what is in everything but name Eton College Chapel, pondering the nature of God whilst the Reverend Pelvey, as Huxley solecistically calls him, reads from the sixth chapter of the Book of Deuteronomy:

And could it be that the Reverend Pelvey, M. A., foghorning away from behind the imperial bird, could it be that he had an answer and a clue? That was hardly believable. Particularly if one knew Mr Pelvey personally. And Gumbril did.

Huxley, who had been a boy at Eton from 1908-11, had returned to teach there in September 1917 (poor eyesight disqualified him for military service). Harold Acton would recall: 'Among the young masters was one who stood out a mile. Walking along the Eton High like a somnambulist, or like a juvenile giraffe that had escaped the zoo, he wore a conspicuous orange scarf that trailed behind him'.

Antic Hay is one of the great comic novels of the 1920s. Evelyn Waugh thought it a supremely happy book, 'Happiness is growing wild for anyone to pick, only the perverse miss it'. There is, however, one obviously perverse character in the book, the witty, blaspheming sexual predator, Coleman:

A young man with a blond fan-shaped beard stood by the table, looking down at them from a pair of bright blue eyes and smiling equivocally and disquietingly as though his mind were full of some nameless and fantastic malice.

Challenged to explain the beard, Coleman makes a sign of the cross and replies:

> Christlike is my behaviour
> Like every good believer
> I imitate the Saviour
> And cultivate the beaver.

Philip Heseltine, on whom the character of Coleman is based, was, indeed, fond of dashing off impromptu verses; in real life, they tended to be mildly obscene limericks on subjects vaguely connected with music. One such limerick appeared in 1925 at the height of the success singer John Goss and pianist Hubert Foss were having with a series of gramophone records of so-called 'sociable music', hymns, folk-songs, sea-shanties, and the like:

> That scandalous pair Goss and Foss
> Once attempted to put it across
>   A girl on a train
>   But their efforts proved vain,
> So Foss tossed off Goss at King's Cross

Others were even more obviously *ad hominem*. When critic Ernest Newman lambasted Heseltine's paper *The Sackbut*, Heseltine publicly dubbed Newman a cuckold:

> Said a critic initialled E. N.:
> 'Why does my wife like young men?'
>   A friend said: 'You fool,
>   Don't you know that the tool
> Is mightier far than the pen?'

Newman eventually forgave Heseltine, posthumously at least. Reviewing a memorial concert which took place at the Wigmore Hall shortly after Heseltine's death in a gas-filled room in December 1930, Newman suggested that the man who could write such exquisite songs as 'Corpus Christi', 'As Dew in Aprille', and 'Balulalow' had 'the root of the matter in him'. 'They are three gems,' he added, 'that will keep his name alive as a composer.'

*

When he first arrived at Eton in September 1908 (the same year as Huxley), Philip Heseltine was a quiet, shy, musically gifted boy in thrall to his widowed but newly married mother, Edith Buckley Jones. He had been placed fourth in the Eton Scholarship list the previous July but the scholarship had been declined. It was felt that he would feel more at home in an Oppidan house than in College; added to which, the socially conscious Mrs Buckley Jones had learned that it was 'not the done thing' for wealthy parents to accept charitable offerings, even from Eton.

By the time Philip arrived at Eton, the school had the nucleus of a first-rate music staff. There was Lloyd himself, the composer Thomas Dunhill, the cellist and chorus-master Edward Mason whose choir had been looked upon with approval by the young Thomas Beecham, and pianist Colin Taylor. It has been said that all any child needs in the course of school life is one inspiring teacher. Philip Heseltine found such a teacher in Colin Taylor. To Philip, he more or less was Eton.

Realising that the boy lacked the wherewithal to become a professional pianist, Taylor concentrated from the outset on widening his musical horizons and extolling the virtues of sightreading as a tried and tested method of musical exploration. Taylor, who died in 1973 at the age of 88, would look back on it all with a certain benign amusement. 'In those days I probably considered myself the deuce of a go-ahead modern, for I was playing and teaching Debussy, Ravel, Schoenberg, Scriabin and the then available Bartók, hot from the press, so to speak.'

At some stage in this process, Philip discovered the music of Delius and was instantly besotted with it. His mother suggested that her brother-in-law, who lived near Delius's French home at Grez-sur-Loing, might be an effective go-between. She even suggested that Delius might be persuaded to visit Eton. It was a rather wild idea but it caused Philip to redouble his efforts over the piano transcription of *Brigg Fair* on which he was working.

In June 1911 the Edward Mason Choir joined forces with the Thomas Beecham Symphony Orchestra for the London première of Delius's *Songs of Sunset*. After lengthy negotiations Taylor persuaded Philip's housemaster, Hubert Brinton, to allow Philip to travel to Paddington where Taylor would collect him and take him to the concert. For Philip it was the red letter day to end all red letter days, the more so when he met Delius during the interval. The only disappointment came on the journey back from Paddington. Thomas Dunhill was on the same train. He told Philip that he had contemplated going to the concert but had spent the evening at White City instead. An evening entirely given over to Delius, he averred, was more than any human being could reasonably be expected to endure.

Philip wrote to his mother describing the concert as 'so beautiful, it almost hurt'. More importantly, he wrote to

Delius, thus starting a correspondence and, more particularly, a friendship that lasted until Philip's death in 1930. The correspondence is rich and wide-ranging, though there were those who came to believe that it was Delius, increasingly isolated and infirm, who was the principal beneficiary of the relationship, not Philip. In his book on Delius, published in 1959, Sir Thomas Beecham observed:

Frederick, once he had escaped from Bradford, not only realised that music was everything on earth to him, but had the iron will to pursue his way towards a definite goal, without hesitations, misgivings, or complaint... Philip was of a quite different type. At that time barely nineteen [seventeen] years of age, and of a mental development which he himself admitted was distinctly backward, he vaguely desired a career with all the intensity of a great longing and a fruitful imagination, but was entirely incapable of either following a fixed course, or doing some of those things which might have expedited the close of a long period of vacillating apprenticeship.

*

It was after Eton and Oxford ('that blasted colony of Hell') that Philip Heseltine vanished and Peter Warlock was born. Philip loved wordplay and littered his manuscripts with bizarre pseudonyms: Apparatus Criticus, Bagwaller, Obricus Scacabarozus, Prosdocimus de Beldamandis, Rab Noolas ('Saloon Bar' backwards: he was one of the pioneers of the 'Real Ale' movement), and Q. Yew. He first used the pseudonym 'Warlock' in November 1916. 'A man in league with the Devil' is one of the definitions offered by the *Oxford English Dictionary* 'and so possessing occult and evil powers; a sorcerer, a wizard; a man who practises witchcraft'.

There were few who knew Heseltine in the 1920s who

doubted the relevance, in part at least, of that definition. Or was it simply that no one really knew what to make of this 'waspish Elizabethan bravo with a courtly air' (Jack Lindsay's phrase) with his passion for beer and cricket, his encyclopaedic knowledge of Elizabethan and Jacobean poetry and music; this spoofer and libertine who indulged in extravagant acrobatics when happy (in the pub, in the Queen's Hall, in the Café Royal, in Piccadilly Circus) and, at a certain stage in a night's drinking, would strip off and run naked through the streets?

D. H. Lawrence, who first met Philip in 1916 and who was later successfully sued (£50 damages with £10 costs) for what the courts adjudged to be the libellous portrait of him as Halliday in *Women in Love*, thought him unformed, incomplete. He wrote to Ottoline Morrell:

Heseltine is here also. I like him, but he seems empty, uncreated... [he] seems as if he were not yet born, as if he consisted only of echoes from the past. But he will perhaps come to being soon: when a new world comes to pass.

He did, but not in the way Lawrence expected or approved. The urge to laugh, criticise, and cajole was too strong. Hubert Brinton had written on his final housemaster's report from Eton, 'Let him find something to *admire uncritically* in everything & his judgment will form on right lines by combining critical faculty with large-heartedness', something Philip did no more than spasmodically. In 1924, we find him busily rescoring 'Old Codger', his send-up of César Franck's Symphony in D minor, for the Savoy Orpheans (piano, banjo, violin, saxophones, trumpets, trombone, and tuba) whilst preparing an hour-long programme for the BBC entitled 'Old

English Ayres and Keyboard Music', a learned programme with a preface, typical of Philip, which might equally have come from the pen of Colin Taylor:

If people would only listen to music without being obsessed with the notion that they will not understand it unless they are 'educated up to it', they would be surprised at the ease with which they understood it and the increase of pleasure they derived from it. It is a fact that some of the very novel music of the present-day often makes an immediate appeal to the plain music-lover... while the professional musician is often unable to free his mind from theoretical preoccupations.

When the South African poet Roy Campbell heard of Philip's death, he paid tribute to him in 'Dedication of a Tree'. It evokes a man

> Who in one hour, resounding, clear, and strong,
> A century of ant-hood far out-glows,
> And burns more sunlight in a single song
> Than they can store against the winter snows.

There was, and remains, more to Warlock than the *Capriol Suite*.

CHAPTER 17

March against the Philistines

Roger Quilter, Henry Ley, Humphrey Lyttelton

The Chapel in which Huxley's Mr Gumbril sat in his oaken stall musing on Life, God and the Reverend Pelvey was about to undergo a significant change. In the summer of 1923, the oak panelling covering the medieval wall paintings was removed and for the first time the organ bellows were electronically (and thus effectively) driven. Luxmoore marvelled:

The change in Chapel by removal of the Stalls is amazing, it looks twice as large, stately, Catholic, austere. the paintings – what is left of them – are as good as Ghirlandaio or the usual good Italian works, better than many.

There were teething troubles with the electricity, but Luxmoore found solace even in this:

Did you hear how 3 Sundays ago the new electric lighting & organ all switched off in the middle of the psalm in Sunday Evensong? the quire went on by heart without a waver. there were 2 little candles at the lectern & the lessons were read & prayers said & the whole service went through & the boys went out orderly in the dark, rather a wonderful test of good feeling & discipline?

In October 1924, Luxmoore saw the completion of another initiative in which he had been involved. In 1914, Arthur Leveson-Gower had written about and acquired the case and pipe-work of a beautiful late eighteenth-century Dutch organ by Mitterreither of Leyden which had been removed from the English church of St Mary's in Rotterdam during demolition.

The organ had been given to Eton which had shown scant interest in this distinguished cadaver until a City man, an Old Etonian by the name of Askew, offered £1,200 (he ended up paying £2,500) to have the organ rebuilt and installed in School Hall where it remains to this day. On 28 October, Luxmoore wrote: 'The organ is finished, enormous 4 manuals up-to-date but the little Rotterdammer is charming when played alone, rather like a harpsichord to a Steinway iron-clad.'[1]

Further work was done on the organ in College Chapel during the 1920s, some of it funded by John Christie. Having spent his youth taking motor cars to pieces, Christie had now developed a fascination with organs. An immediate priority at Glyndebourne was to be the creation of an Organ Room, for which he had consulted Hill & Son, builders of the organ in College Chapel. Shortly afterwards, he acquired a stake in the business.[2]

The inheritor of the fruits of these (to sober-suited folk, no doubt somewhat peculiar) initiatives by Luxmoore and Christie was the 39-year-old Henry Ley, who succeeded Basil Johnson as Precentor in 1926. A Devonian who had been a chorister at St George's, Windsor, Ley was one of the most gifted organists of his generation. Appointed organist of Christ Church, Oxford whilst still an undergraduate, he had

1 A letter from Luxmoore to the *Eton College Chronicle* on 4 October, 1924 points out that the Precentor, Basil Johnson, had been doubly remiss during the organ's unveiling when he revealed the anonymous donor's identity whilst making no mention of Leveson-Gower.

2 Christie being Christie, he did not confine himself to church organs. The firm won contracts to install organs in the Brighton Dome, the Regal Cinema, Marble Arch and the Gaumont Theatre in Paris. An off-the-shelf speciality was the 'Christie Organ Unit'. This came complete with 'Sleigh Bells' and 'Crockery Smash' effects. Prices ranged from £1,145 all the way up to £4,594 (the 'for use in the tropics' model).

been Director of Music at Radley before going on to teach at the Royal College of Music. It was impossible not to like Ley. A small, rotund man, he had a kindly disposition and an infectious laugh. His extra-musical passions were the highways and byways of England, on which he and his wife were amateur experts, and railways, an enthusiasm attested to by the presence in his Eton home of the name-plate of a Great Western locomotive.

For all the brilliance of his keyboard playing (the violinist Jelly d'Arányi was astonished by his playing of his own transcription of the orchestral part of Ravel's *Tzigane*), Ley was an odd choice as Precentor. Good choral conductors don't always make good orchestral conductors. Ley's problem was that he was neither. Ironically, it was visits by the orchestra of Ley's former school, Radley, which most put Eton to shame in the 1930s. The Eton orchestra's so-called 'showpiece' in Ley's time was Ravel's controversial smash-hit *Bolero* (1928) but even the orchestra's most loyal members were ready to concede that its performances were rarely less than rackety.

In the fullness of time, Ley's deputy, Mervyn Bruxner, founded a smaller, less ambitious but more expert 'Junior Orchestra'. Unlike the school orchestra, this was closed to masters and their wives, a decision which caused a good deal of ill will. 'What a splendid idea! I do hope I can join. When is the first rehearsal? ... Oh, well, if I'm not wanted ... ' was the general drift of most conversations, further widening the gulf that already existed between the academic staff and the shadowy denizens of the Music Schools. Bruxner's predecessor, Albert Mellor, a full-time member of staff, had been one of several Eton musicians who routinely touched their hats to Eton masters in the street. Little wonder that many of the peripatetic music teachers carried on their shoulders, not chips, but copses, plantations, and in the case of Mr Geoffrey Leeds, who taught at Eton for more than fifty years, an entire forest of resentment.

Unusually for a Precentor, Ley taught a good deal but his teaching, like his conducting, was endearingly shambolic. Since he never remembered to call the roll (if he called it at all) until the end of a music appreciation class, most boys merely crawled into the back of the room on all fours towards the conclusion of proceedings. Those who did attend had to put up with the fact that, like many distinguished musicians, Ley was largely incapable of operating a gramophone. Humphrey Lyttelton, who had been born and brought up in Eton, has left a particularly vivid description of Ley and the gramophone:

It was an early, winding model which looked like a commode and sounded like nothing on earth. The turntable had a persistent squeak which intruded even when the music was *fortissimo*. Furthermore, it revolved so unevenly that all sustained passages fluctuated mournfully like a wartime siren. Whenever some subtlety of composition needed emphasis, the Doctor would accompany the gramophone at the piano. But as he never bothered to synchronise the speed-control, the two instruments were always a semi-tone apart in tuning. Henry Ley knew this, and commented on it. But he never discovered how to remedy it, nor did it seem to worry him at all. Even when he was lecturing, he used to stand at the piano with his hands on the keyboard, absent-mindedly drowning his own words with rambling chords.

*

In November 1928, another 'Concert by Old Etonians composed by Old Etonians' was staged. In addition to works by Arne, Parry, Butterworth and F. S. Kelly, it featured music by two living composers, Roger Quilter, who cried off sick shortly before the concert, and Victor Hely-Hutchinson who arranged and rehearsed the event.

Hely-Hutchinson was the son of Sir Walter Hely-Hutchinson, the last Governor of Cape Colony in South Africa. Nowadays, he is best remembered for his fine *Carol Symphony* and his Handel parody *Old Mother Hubbard*. He made his greatest impact, however, as a musical administrator. In 1926, he joined Reith's BBC (Reith had a weakness for Etonians) as an adviser and music producer. His advice seems to have been fairly sound. An internal memorandum concerning the auditioning of the 19-year-old Benjamin Britten in June 1933 states: 'I do whole-heartedly subscribe to the general opinion that Mr Britten is the most interesting new arrival since Walton, and I feel we should watch his work very carefully.'

In 1944, Hely-Hutchinson became the BBC's Director of Music, innovative but pleasingly down-to-earth. Typically, he reminds producers that broadcast concerts are for the benefit of listeners not studio audiences (a recent transmission from NBC in New York had been held up whilst the conductor sent for a new collar-stud). At the same time, he advises that musical considerations alone must determine whether the BBC should broadcast Richard Strauss's new Oboe Concerto. The fact that Strauss had been 'on the wrong side in the recent hostilities' was not an issue.

As Director of Music, Hely-Hutchinson was closely involved in the planning and launching of the BBC Third Programme, the high-water mark, culturally and intellectually, of public service broadcasting in Britain in the twentieth century. Sadly, he did not live to see the idea through to completion. He died in 1947, at the unexpectedly early age of 45.

Not untypically, the man the BBC chose to replace him succeeded in sowing dissension and strife throughout the organisation within months of taking up his appointment.

★

Roger Quilter was represented at the 1928 concert mainly by his Shakespeare settings, the music for which he is best remembered. Several of the songs had featured in the earlier concert of music by Old Etonians in 1910 which the young Philip Heseltine had attended. Three years later, he wrote: '[Quilter's] setting of Shakespeare's "O, Mistress Mine" is the most exquisite and lovely lyric I know... one feels absolute perfection in its three brief pages.' He would later send a copy of one of his own songs to Quilter with the inscription: 'To R.Q. without whom there could have been no P. W.'

If any musician can be said to conform to the idea of the Old Etonian gentleman composer – the stylish amateur, charming and a little aloof – it is Quilter. His father was Sir Cuthbert Quilter, Bt, founder of the National Telephone Company and, for many years, M.P. for Sudbury in Suffolk. The family home was Bawdsey Manor near Felixstowe, a background about which Quilter always felt vaguely guilty. In a letter in 1911, he wrote: 'I've given up hoping to be an artist myself – I have the English rich upper-middle-class blood in my veins too much, I'm not strong enough to fight it.'

After Eton, he had studied in Frankfurt with Iwan Knorr whose pupils included Henry Balfour Gardiner, Percy Grainger and Hans Pfitzner. Song was his *forte*. He was a slow worker but a fastidious craftsman which explains why his songs were readily accepted by leading singers of the time:

Clara Butt, John Coates, Gervase Elwes, Harry Plunket Greene, Nellie Melba, Maggie Teyte.

Too fragile and too old to fight, Quilter involved himself in charitable work during the First World War, an activity which required tact as well as musicianship. After a song recital in which he had played the piano for his companion the tenor Mark Raphael,[3] Quilter was approached by a society hostess. 'And are *you* fond of music, too?' she demanded, apparently oblivious of the fact that he had been playing the piano for the past hour. Quilter replied that he was not averse to the art.

When Gervase Elwes was killed in a railway accident while on tour in the United States, Quilter and friends set up a 'Gervase Elwes Memorial Fund', the origin, as it later proved, of the 'Musicians Benevolent Fund'. He also continued pursuing private charitable giving in his familiar self-depreciatory way. 'I can't think of any better way of spending my money than helping to get your name better known in the world,' he told Percy Grainger, whose publishing costs he was proposing to subsidise.

To those who did not know him, Quilter must have seemed enviably at ease with himself, yet he continued to suffer both from ill-health and a persistent fear that his homosexuality would be publicly exposed. There is, indeed, a homoerotic element in some of his music but it was buried deep within, well away from the gaze of the Director of Public Prosecutions. Curiously, one of his most obviously erotic songs, his

---

3 Quilter recorded 17 of his songs with Mark Raphael for English Columbia. Like Quilter, Raphael was a musician of taste, sensibility and wide learning who made a virtue of his limitation (a dryish tenor voice). As befits a star pupil of the great German tenor Raimund von Zur Mühlen, Raphael's diction was second to none. This quality alone renders his Quilter recordings nonpareil.

setting of Tennyson's 'Now sleeps the crimson petal', was a favourite song of the mother of Benjamin Britten.[4]

Anyone hearing Quilter's celebrated *A Children's Overture* might reasonably conclude that he is the English Humperdinck. He might well have been. The overture was written in 1911 as the prelude to the faery play *Where the Rainbow Ends* which was being staged at London's Savoy Theatre by children from the Italia Conti Stage School. ('I like your music, Mr Quilter!' announced one of the children, the 12-year-old Noël Coward.) Sadly, there is no equivalent in Quilter's output to *Hänsel und Gretel*. The nearest he came to a successful stage show was *Julia* (Covent Garden, 1936) of which nowadays only the Waldteufel-like waltz-sequence 'Rosmé' is occasionally played. Percy Grainger was also way wide of the mark when he described Quilter's *Three English Dances* as 'your warm roaring seething loving stuff on a nice billowy band'. Quilter's music is tuneful and charming to a fault; it never roars, nor does it billow or seethe.

His own musical tastes were as unaffected as the man. He once said, 'I am glad to say I can appreciate any kind of music which is sincere and vital – from Bach to good ragtime. I enjoy immensely the music of *Patience*, and can also keenly relish Stravinsky's *Petrushka*'. Alas, he never wrote anything remotely as good as either *Patience* or *Petrushka*. Even when he was invited to contribute a tableau (choreography by Massine) based on Hogarth's *The Rake's Progress* for Charles B. Cochran's revue *On with the Dance* in 1925, the music remained imperturbably genteel.

4 Britten's own setting of the poem, an altogether more passionate and graphic piece than Quilter's, was intended for inclusion in his *Serenade for Tenor, Horn and Strings* but was withdrawn before the first performance. It remained unpublished during Britten's lifetime.

Dyson's in the High Street, where Brian Howard had acted out his Nijinsky impersonations, continued to do a roaring trade at a time when gramophones and wirelesses were banned from boys' rooms. Humphrey Lyttelton would recall:

One day, one of our group came back from having flu in the school Sanatorium in a state of great excitement, having heard a record on the wireless by Louis Armstrong which had knocked him sideways. The tune was 'Basin Street Blues', and we went straight up to the record shop to order it. Service there was leisurely and we had to wait several weeks for the record to arrive. By this time we were in such a state of excited anticipation after our friend's build-up that anything but the greatest and most dramatic jazz record of all time would have been a disappointment. But Louis Armstrong's 'Basin Street Blues' is just that. And after playing it fifteen times we tottered out into the daylight with the incredulous stunned expressions of the newly converted.

Later, they found it was quicker to order records from the Windsor branch of Dyson's, though token acquisitions were necessary in the High Street to keep the listening booth option going.

Many a hot summer's day, when our parents and masters fondly believed us to be taking healthy outdoor exercise, we were crammed, seven or eight at a time, in the unhygienic little cubicle listening to jazz. The first Saturday in every month was a red letter day for us. The new monthly record releases were out, and we used to dash off immediately after the last morning class to Dyson's on Windsor Hill to buy them up. While Mrs Dyson tried in vain to keep law and order, we crawled about over the floor and the shelves and in between the legs of other customers, whooping with excitement at every find.

Sixty years on, it is virtually impossible to buy classical records, let alone anything as esoteric as traditional jazz, in

Eton or Windsor. I remember the look of dismay on the face of a Colleger from the late 1970s when he saw the old Eton Organ Centre – the place where he had acquired many of his most treasured LPs – standing empty.[5]

Lyttelton and his friends were clearly a law unto themselves but music-loving loners had a rather harder row to hoe in Eton in the 1930s, especially after the arrival of Claude Elliott as Head Master in 1933. Whether Elliott said all, or any, of the things attributed to him it is impossible to ascertain. Attributed remarks range from 'Would you be seen about with musical people?' to an interest in music being 'coterminous with the fleshpots of effeminacy'. When a boy's aunt went, on behalf of his mother, to inform Elliott that the boy wanted to pursue music professionally, Elliott is said to have replied 'I'd sooner have heard that he'd taken to drink'.

Such remarks, which Wilfrid Blunt and others would relish reporting in their memoirs, look grim on the page. In reality, Elliott took no pride in his lack of musicality. A modest man, able and privately affable, he seems to have developed a pleasing line in self-mockery where music was concerned. A request to stage an informal performance of *Messiah* was greeted with the words: 'I would forbid it if I could think of a reason. Unfortunately, I cannot.' Asked how he endured a full-blown choral concert, he confessed that he went over in his mind, step by step, memorable mountain climbs. And if he wearied of that? 'I contemplate my sins.'

Elliott was not alone in being naturally suspicious of musicians. The Duke of Windsor is said to have remarked about the future Director of the Edinburgh Festival, George Harewood, 'It's very odd about George and music. You know,

5 It has since been turned into a beauty salon.

his parents were quite normal.' (Harewood's father was far from normal but that is another story.) A number of house-masters at the time were openly hostile to the arts in a way which was widely accepted before the sea-change which over-took English Public Schools in the 1950s and 1960s. An old Eton story runs:

M'TUTOR: Now I want to know what you were doing in the Music Schools this evening.
BOY: We were playing the Rachmaninov Concertos, Sir.
M'TUTOR: Yes, but I want to know what you were DOING!

Individual masters, and that most redoubtable of house-masters' wives, Grizel Hartley, would occasionally hold 'gramophone evenings' but it was Mervyn Bruxner's Gramo-phone Society which effectively saved the day. Bruxner's own conversion to the gramophone had come about when a boy arrived with music for 'Non più andrai' from Mozart's *Le nozze di Figaro*, an aria Bruxner had not previously heard. He resolved then and there to expand his musical horizons. At the same time, he realised there were boys in the school (hundreds, it later turned out) who liked music but who, for one reason or another, had no means of hearing it.

The format Bruxner devised was ingenious. Gramophone Society meetings were in two parts. The first was largely given over to lighter fare and always included some live music-making, designed to humanise the proceedings. In the second half, a longer work would be played: a symphony, a concerto or an extract from an opera. For this, he had a BBC-style twin-turntable, specially built by a technically-minded colleague, which allowed him to play works continuously rather than in the four-and-a-half minute sections 78 rpm sides demanded.

He also provided rather more background information in what we must assume was the same artfully (or possibly genuinely) unintellectual manner he adopts in his book *Letters to a Musical Boy* which Oxford University Press published in 1940 and which was reprinted in 1954 with some additional remarks about Lennox Berkeley (the Divertimento for Chamber Orchestra warmly commended), Britten (much admired) and Tippett ('difficult but deep in feeling'). Preparing the gramophone recitals must have been a time-consuming task, especially where opera was concerned. Deaf, by his own confession, to the charms of Verdi and Puccini, and dubious about Wagner, Bruxner spent many a long hour seeking out palatable extracts.[6]

The gramophone has its disadvantages. When Sir Thomas Beecham and his dazzlingly gifted London Philharmonic Orchestra appeared in School Hall in 1937, their rendering of the 'Nocturne' and 'Scherzo' from Mendelssohn's *A Midsummer Night's Dream* music was said by the *Eton College Chronicle* to have been something of a disappointment to those familiar with Toscanini's New York Philharmonic recording. When the excellent Boyd Neel Orchestra presumed to play Mozart's *Eine kleine Nachtmusik* at a similar concert, reference was made in the *Chronicle* to the superior accomplishments of Bruno Walter and the Vienna Philharmonic.

It is to the credit of Bruxner and, to a less extent, the somewhat more circumspect Ley that an increasing number of famous musicians visited Eton during the 1930s. Beecham's

---

6 In *Letters to a Musical Boy*, Bruxner writes of Wagner: 'Of all the composers, he is, I think, the most astonishing, the most gigantic, the most thrilling – and the most boring!'. Rossini put the same idea rather more elegantly: '*Monsieur Wagner a de beaux moments, mais de mauvais quart-d'heures*'.

two concerts were an evident highlight, though the programme of the second was considered too 'highbrow' by the
Chronicle,[7] which also ventured to suggest that at the time of
the first concert in February 1936 the majority of boys had
gone to see Sir Thomas rather than to hear the music. And
why not? Bernard Levin, whose uncle played in the London
Philharmonic in the 1930s, recalls being awe-struck as a child
by the orchestra's roster of great conductors: Beecham,
van Beinum, de Sabata, Furtwängler, Bruno Walter. As he
would note at the time of the London Philharmonic's fiftieth
anniversary in 1982: 'A youth just beginning his journey into
music must have such stars to steer by; he must also have suns
and moons, in the form of the composers to whom he gives a
similar allegiance'.

Whatever the boys' motives for attending, the first of the
two Beecham concerts offered a characteristically seductive
programme.[8] As for the conducting, 'Sir Thomas can mould a
musical phrase in his hands like a potter moulds a vase', The
Chronicle poetically if somewhat ungrammatically enthused.
Bruxner remembers that at dinner at Henry Ley's afterwards
Beecham was unexpectedly modest and courteous; it was his
principal oboist, Leon Goossens, who held court.

Musicians who appeared at Eton in the 1930s and early 1940s
included violinists Jelly d'Arányi and Ida Haendel, pianists
Myra Hess and Benno Moiseiwitsch, and singers Roy

7 Rimsky-Korsakov *May Night Overture*; Dvorak *Legends in G* and *G minor*;
Mendelssohn 'Nocturne' and 'Scherzo' from incidental music to *A Midsummer
Night's Dream*; Haydn Symphony No. 104, London; Elgar *Enigma Variations*; Berlioz
Hungarian March from *La Damnation de Faust*.
8 Rossini *La scala di seta* Overture; Delius *On Hearing the First Cuckoo in Spring, Sum-
mer Night on the River*; Mozart Symphony No. 40; Wagner *Siegfried Idyll*; Beecham
Handel arrangements.

Henderson and Paul Robeson. Robeson so astounded the audience, they demanded encores after virtually every song. As a consequence, he completed barely more than half his programme. Asked afterwards who his singing teachers had been, he said he hadn't had any. After booking a single lesson – 'just to see if the voice was O. K.' – he trod his own path to fame and fortune.

Some artists fared better than others in the unpredictable School Hall acoustic which a committee of so-called experts made a somewhat alarming attempt to rectify in the late 1930s. Their suggested solution was the lining of the walls with asbestos. As the work was proceeding, a sceptical onlooker enquired how such treatment could possibly be expected to improve the acoustics. 'Acoustics?' said the workman, witheringly, taking up a lump of wet plaster, 'Why, this is the acoustic wot I'm puttin' on now.'

Ley and Elliott countenanced official concerts but, if Blunt's memoirs are to be believed, there was suppression, too. For warriors against the philistines such as Blunt, Ley's remark to Elliott in masters' Chambers, 'I think we've scotched that one, Head Master!' became a representative text.

Another such story tells how shortly after the start of the Second World War two boys engaged the pianist Louis Kentner to play at Eton. While Ley asked around, trying to ascertain who precisely Louis Kentner was (an improbable detail), one obstacle after another was placed in the boys' way. Having been warned that the recital must cover its costs, they were informed an hour before it was due to begin that no more than thirty people might attend because of 'blackout regulations'. The sight of flowers on stage is said to have rendered Ley apoplectic ('Flowers for a man!'). Meanwhile, even as Ley was ordering the return of the flowers to Luxmoore's Garden, the boys' Dame, who had been a tower of strength in helping organise the event, was summoned by her housemaster's wife and told that, since she and her husband were going out to drinks, the Dame must forego the recital in order to look after the house.[9] On another occasion, it is said, permission was given to a boy to travel to Slough to hear the pianist Solomon, on condition that he was chaperoned by his Dame and they both left at the interval.

Perhaps the oddest of these tales concerns a winner of the school Divinity Prize who was discovered to have used the prize money to buy, not books, but Furtwängler's 1937 HMV recording of Beethoven's Fifth Symphony, revered then and still revered now. He was ordered, not unreasonably perhaps, to return the records to the shop in the High Street and buy books instead. Rather less reasonably, he was required to stay behind for a day at the end of term to swab floors.

*

Henry Ley survived as Precentor until 1945, though only just. On the evening of 4 December, 1940 a high explosive bomb fell on the centre of Savile House, destroying the dining room which the Leys were about to enter. It seems that the Precentor's fancy had been taken by a joke in *Punch* which he had been determined to share with Mrs Ley before they went in to dinner.

9 The *Eton College Chronicle* carries no mention of the recital, which suggests either that the story is a fabrication or that official disfavour was every bit as strong as Blunt's informant claimed it was.

In 1968, Eton closed its Choir School. The reasons – falling rolls, rising costs, the uncertain attitude of the 1960s towards organised religion and, it has to be said, the antagonism shown by some members of the community to what, in Barnby's day, would have been called 'the Sunday opera' – were complex. As Henry James observed to Edward Elgar after missing him at a reception, 'It was a complicated and scattered scene & one wasn't one's master'.

The Provost and Fellows were, however, the masters of one aspect of the situation. If the Choir School was to close, the money saved should be devoted, in its entirety, to music at Eton. It proved to be a momentous decision. In the years which followed, the scholarships which Eton now provided attracted a succession of brilliant young musicians, many of them from families who would not otherwise have imagined, or possibly desired, that their sons might one day go out into the world as Old Etonians.

The renovation of College Chapel rendered necessary by the joint ministration of German bombs and the death-watch beetle brought the building closer than it had ever been to a state Henry VI might have approved. And now music, too, was entering an era of particular achievement.

Eton greeted the new millennium with a chapel choir as skilled and eloquent as any since the years of the Choirbook itself; with a collection of organs and boy organists which

Hayne and Barnby, Lloyd and Ley would have attended to slack-jawed in admiration; with speaking winds and a chamber orchestra whose strings are capable of ravishing sense. Hubert Parry was a phenomenon in his day but, in the millennium year itself, barely an eyebrow was raised when the President of the Eton Society, Keeper of Association [Captain of Football], and middle-order batsman at Lord's [1] took his leave of Eton as soloist in the Dvorak *Cello Concerto*.

[1] Matthew Lowe.

ACKNOWLEDGEMENTS

Research for this was book was mainly carried out in the Rare Books and Music Reading Room of the British Library in London but I also owe a debt of gratitude to the Eton College Librarian, Michael Meredith, and the Eton College Library Administrator, Nick Baker, who allowed me access to the Eton Choirbook and who pointed me towards material in the College's possession which I might otherwise have missed, and to Selma Thomas and her staff in the Eton School Library. The finished typescript was read by Nigel Jaques, a mine of information on all matters Etonian, whose comments and suggestions were characteristically vivid and perspicacious. I am indebted to Charles Mitchell-Innes for reading some of the early chapters, to James Bruxner for the loan of his father's unpublished memoir of music at Eton in the 1930s, and to Alastair Sampson for providing me with rare copies of Quilter recordings. Since it was my hope from the outset to have this published, not as a trade book, but as a private press monograph, it might not have happened at all had it not been for the interest and expertise of my designer and publisher, Simon Rendall. An early draft of the book was completed during the summer of 2001 in the villa of my parents-in-law in Lanzarote, an even more agreeable location in which to write, dare I say it, than Eton itself.

Acton, Harold *Memoirs of an Aesthete* (London, 1948)

Amory, Mark *Lord Berners: The Last Eccentric* (London, 1998)

Anderson, Robert *Edward Elgar* (London, 1993)

Anon. *An Elegy on the death of The Guardian Outwitted, an opera, written and composed by T. A. Arne* (London, 1765)

— [O. E.] *Eton under Hornby* (London, 1910)

— *The Opera Il Penseroso [i.e. the operation of birching]* (London, c. 1790)

— *A Plain and True Narrative of the Differences between Messrs B----s and the members of the Musical-Club, holden at the Old-Cock, in Halifax, in a letter to a friend* (1767)

Bairstow, V.M. (ed.) *Memories of Eton College Choir School* (Eton, 1993)

Barlow, Michael *Whom the Gods Love: The Life and Music of George Butterworth* (London, 1997)

Beecham, Sir Thomas *Frederick Delius* (London, 1958)

Bensoniana and Cornishiana, eds. J. A. Gere and Logan Pearsall Smith (Settrington, 1999)

Berners, Lord *A Distant Prospect* (London, 1945)

Blunt, Wilfrid *John Christie of Glyndebourne* (London, 1968)

— *Slow on the Feather* (Salisbury, 1986)

Bridges, Robert *About Hymns* (London, 1912)

— *A Practical Discourse on some Principles of Hymn-Singing* (Oxford, 1901)

— *Ode for the Bicentenary Commemoration of Henry Purcell… and a preface on the musical setting of poetry* (London, 1896)

— *The Yattendon Hymnal*, 4 vols (London, 1899)

Browning, Oscar *Memories of Sixty Years at Eton, Cambridge, and Elsewhere* (London, 1910)

Bruxner, Mervyn *A Hundred Years of Music Making: A History of the Windsor and Eton Choral Society 1841-1941* (Windsor, 1941)

— *Letters to a Musical Boy* (London, 1940 / R1954)

— 'Eton as a beak', ch.17 of typescript of unpublished memoir

Burney, Charles *An Account of the Musical Performances in Westminster Abbey and the Pantheon. In Commemoration of Handel* (London, 1785)

— *Memoirs of Dr Charles Burney 1726-1769*, eds. Slava Klima, Garry Bowers and Kerry S. Grant (Nebraska, 1988)

Burrows, Donald *Handel* (London, 1994)

Byard, Herbert 'Robert Bridges: Church Musician', *Music and Letters*, LIII, i, 1972

Caldwell, John *The Oxford History of English Music*, Vol.1, From the beginnings to *c*.1715 (Oxford, 1991)

Card, Tim *Eton Established* (London, 2001)

— *Eton Renewed* (London, 1994)

Connolly, Cyril *The Condemned Playground* (London, 1945)

— *Enemies of Promise* (London, 1938)

— *A Romantic Friendship: The Letters of Cyril Connolly to Noel Blakiston* (London, 1975)

Dean, Winton *Handel's Dramatic Oratorios and Masques* (Oxford, 1959)

De-la-Noy, Michael *Eddy: The Life of Edward Sackville-West* (London, 1988)

Deutsch, Otto Erich *Handel: A Documentary Biography* (London, 1955)

Dexter, Keri *The Provision of Choral Music at St George's Chapel, Windsor Castle and Eton College c. 1640-1733* (University of London, 2000, unpublished thesis)

Dibble, Jeremy C. *Hubert H. Parry: His Life and Music* (Oxford, 1992)

Dictionary of National Biography, from earliest times to 1900, eds. Leslie Stephen and Sidney Lee (London, 1921-2)

Elgar, Edward *Elgar and his Publishers: Letters of a Creative Life*, ed. J. N. Moore (2 vols, Oxford, 1987)

— *Letters of a Lifetime*, ed. J. N. Moore (Oxford, 1990)

Eton College Chronicle (Eton, 1863-1940)

Etoniana (Eton, 1904-75)

Fellowes, Edmund *English Cathedral Music* (London, 1969)

Fergusson, Bernard *Eton Portrait* (London, 1937)

Foster, Myles *Anthems and Anthem Composers* (London, 1901)

The Gentleman's Magazine (London, 1731-1868)

Graves, Charles L. *Hubert Parry: His Life and Works* (London, 1926)

Gray, Cecil *Peter Warlock: A Memoir of Philip Heseltine* (London, 1934)

Gray, Thomas *Correspondence of Thomas Gray*, eds. Paget Toynbee and Leonard Whibley (Oxford, 1971)

Green, Henry *Pack my Bag* (London, 1940)

Grierson, Mary *Donald Francis Tovey* (Oxford, 1952)

Hackett, Maria *A Voice from the Tomb: seriously addressed to all Etonians who revere the memory of the Founder* (London, 1868)

Hawkins, Sir John *An Account of the Institution and Progress of the Academy of Ancient Music* (London, 1770)

Hollis, Christopher *Eton* (London, 1960)

Horner, Burnham *Life and Works of Dr Arne* (London, 1893)

Huxley, Aldous *Antic Hay* (London, 1923)

— *Letters of Aldous Huxley*, ed. Grover Smith (London, 1969)

James, M. R. *Eton and King's* (London, 1926)

Langley, Hubert *Doctor Arne* (London, 1938)

Lubbock, Percy *Shades of Eton* (London, 1929)

Luxmoore, H. E. *Letters of H. E. Luxmoore*, ed. A. B. Ramsay (Cambridge, 1929)

Lyttelton, Edward *Memories and Hopes* (London, 1925)

Lyttelton, Humphrey *I Play as I Please: The Memoirs of an Old Etonian Trumpeter* (London, 1954)

Mackenzie, Compton *My Record of Music* (London, 1955)

Mackenzie, Faith Compton *William Cory* (London, 1950)

Marsden, Jonathan 'Georgian Cliveden', *Cliveden* (National Trust, London, 1993)

Marsh, Edward *A Number of People* (London, 1939)

Martindale, A. N. R. *The Early History of the Choir of Eton College Chapel* (Oxford, 1971)

Maxwell-Lyte, Sir Henry *History of Eton College 1440-1910* (4th edition, London, 1911)

Mellers, Wilfrid *Harmonious Meeting* (London, 1965)

— 'From gilded chapel to the village street: explorations of three contrasted works by William Cornysh', *Choir and Organ*, Vol.8 no.6, Nov/Dec 2000

Mellor, Albert *Music and Musicians of Eton College* (Eton, 1929)

Moore, Jerrold Northrop *Edward Elgar: A Creative Life* (Oxford, 1984)

Morell, Thomas *The Use and Importance of Music in the Sacrifice of Thanksgiving* (London, 1747)

Music in Eighteenth-Century England, eds. Christopher Hogwood and Richard Luckett (Cambridge, 1983)

Newsome, David *On the Edge of Paradise: A. C. Benson: the Diarist* (London, 1980)

Newton, Ivor *At the Piano* (London, 1966)

Nichols, John *Literary Anecdotes of the Eighteenth Century* (9 vols, London, 1812-15 / R New York, 1966)

Ollard, Richard *An English Education* (London, 1982)

Parke, William *Musical Memoirs* (London, 1830)

Parker, Eric (ed.) *Floreat: An Eton Anthology* (London, 1923)

Parry, Ernest Gambier *Annals of an Eton House* (London, 1907)

Parry, Hubert 'An Eton Boy's Diary 1864-1866', *Etoniana*, 103 (1946), pp. 33-40; 104 (1947), pp. 49-57

Radcliffe, Philip *E. J. Dent: A Centenary Memoir* (Rickmansworth, 1976)

Rainbow, Bernarr *The Choral Revival in the Anglican Church 1839-1872* (Oxford, 1970)

Sackville-West, Edward *Inclinations* (London, 1949)

— *Piano Quintet* (London, 1925)

— *The Rescue: A Melodrama for Broadcasting based on Homer's Odyssey* (London, 1945)

Salt, Henry *Memories of Bygone Eton* (London, 1928)

Scholes, Percy (ed.) *The Mirror of Music 1844-1944*, 2 vols (London, 1947)

Smith, Barry *Peter Warlock: The Life of Philip Heseltine* (Oxford, 1994)

Sterry, Sir Wasey *Annals of Eton College* (London, 1898)

— *The Eton College Register (1441-1698)* (Eton, 1943)

Thistlethwaite, N. J *Organs at Eton* (Eton, 1987)

Tovey, Sir Donald *Walter Parratt* (Oxford, 1941)

Vaughan Williams, Ursula *R.V. W: A Biography of Ralph Vaughan Williams* (Oxford, 1964)

Wilkinson, C. A. *Reminiscences of Eton (Keate's Time)* (London, 1888)

Williamson, Magnus *The Eton Choirbook: its institutional and historical background* (University of Oxford, 1995, unpublished thesis)

— 'Pictura et Scriptura: the Eton Choirbook and its
iconographical content', *Early Music*, xxviii/3, 8/2000

Wolffe, Bertram *Henry VI* (London, 1981)

Wortham H.E. *Victorian Eton and Cambridge. Being the Life and Times of Oscar Browning* (London, 1927)

INDEX

Acton, Harold 138-9, 143, 148
Ainger, A. C. 75, 87
Alexandra of Denmark, queen-
 consort of Edward VII 101
Algarotti, Francesco 31
Alington, Cyril 144-5
Allen, Hugh 122, 124
Armstrong, Louis 163
Armstrong, Thomas 130
Arne, Thomas 23-9, 116, 158
Arnold, Malcolm 40
Arnold, Thomas 57
Arthur, eldest son of Henry VII 12
Auber, Daniel 52
Austen Leigh, E. C. 75-6, 146

Babington Smith, Henry 15
Bach Choir 58, 60
Bach, J. C. 38
Bach, J. S. 39, 60, 103, 111, 117, 118, 131n,
 134, 162
Balanchine, George 134
Baldwin, John 14
Balfour, Arthur 75n
Baring, Maurice 146
Barnby, Joseph 81-7, 118
Barrie, J. M. 107
Barrington-Kennett, V. A. 124
Bartók, Bela 134, 151
Bates, Joah 39, 40-8
Bates, Sarah 48
Battie, William 33
Beatrice, Princess, fifth daughter of
 Queen Victoria 99
Beecham, Thomas 134-5, 150, 151, 166-7
Beethoven, Ludwig van 67, 73, 117, 118,
 127, 132, 141, 169
Bekynton, Thomas 1
Benson, A. C. 28, 93, 97-105, 106, 115n,
 128, 146

Benson, E. W. 97
Benson, F. R. 60
Bentinck, Morven Cavendish 139
Berkeley, Lennox 166
Berlioz, Hector 86, 167n
Berners, Gerald Tyrwhitt-Wilson,
 14th Baron 109, 127-35, 146
Binfield, John 57
Blake, William 28, 71, 136-7
Blakiston, Noel 146
Blow, John 21, 22
Blunt, Wilfrid 164, 168
Bost, Henry 4
Boyce, William 82-3
Boyd Neel Orchestra 166
Bradfield College 57
Brahms, Johannes 88, 117, 134, 141
Bridges, Robert 55, 68, 70, 109-12, 136
Bridgewater, Mr 55
Brinton, Hubert 151, 153
Britten, Benjamin 134, 141, 159, 162, 166
Brooke, Rupert 140n
Browne, John 6, 10, 11-12
Browning, Oscar 59, 67, 73-7, 80, 85, 88,
 146
Bruxner, Mervyn 157, 165-6
Burney, Charles 24, 25, 46-8
Burney, Fanny 25
Busoni, Ferruccio 142
Butler, William 13
Butt, Clara 100, 105-7, 133, 161
Butterworth, George 107, 109, 121-6,
 133, 146, 158
Byrd, William 5, 22, 39
Byron, Robert 138

Campbell, Roy 154
Chabrier, Emmanuel 134
Cheltenham College 57
Child, William 22

178